Jordan Silver

Table of Contents

Chapter ONE

LAURIE

"Garret, Dmitri, get over here; no stop that, come on guys work with mom huh." Whatever possessed me to think I could do this?

I have a crap load of laundry waiting to be done, a house that looks like a hurricane sideswiped it, and what am I doing? Spending my Saturday morning in the park with my boys, that's what.

Why? Because mommy is a pushover that's why, and when they begged so sweetly to go swingy what could I do?

They've heard the word no so often in their young lives already it's good to be able to give them this. The park is still free thank heavens, because money was tight.

The dead beat who'd inseminated me has been long gone. Not that I blamed him completely. What eighteen-year old wanted to hang around for that?

Especially when the girl you knocked up was the sixteen-year old daughter of the local police chief, yikes!

Now the twins are three years old and into everything. We were barely making it, what with me trying to finish school while holding down a full time job.

Daycare was almost as much as my weekly paycheck, and government assistance was a joke.

My poor dad tries to help out as much as he can, but there isn't much he can do on his salary. Kids are expensive little bundles of joy.

I wasn't complaining though, having the boys had changed my life in a way I hadn't planned for, but each day got easier and the joys were outgrowing the fears and doubts.

I finally caught up to them, as they were about to pet this humongous dog that was almost as tall as me. Holy...

"Hey kid, you might not want to do that." They both stopped at the gruff command from the menacing looking guy that I'd missed, sitting on the park bench.

The dog growled low in his throat and I eased forward to get between it and my boys.

"Gunther cut that shit out." He remained seated on the bench while that thing that was posing as a dog had my kids trapped.

"Maybe you want to get up and grab your dog before he mauls my kids?" Was this guy for real?

"Maybe you want to teach your damn kids to keep their hands to themselves."

What the.... He turned that face my way and just wow. Figures, anyone that hot had to have major flaws, and one of his seemed to be being an asshole.
"Listen you jerk off, they're just kids; kids do stuff like that."

"Don't feed me your shit lady, my dog bite into one of your little darlings I'll be knee deep in law suits and bullshit."

"Watch your mouth in front of my kids, what's your problem anyway?"

"People; too many of the fuckers on the planet; more specifically annoying ass people like you, who can never accept when they're wrong. Now would you please get your damn spawns out of here? You're mucking up my morning routine."

"That's it." I didn't care that he was at least a good foot taller, it didn't matter that he looked like he'd chewed nails for breakfast either.

Right now, at this very moment, he was the embodiment of everything I hated. Like the asshole supervisor who was being a dick because I refused to sleep with his slimy ass.

Or the nasty ass customers who came into the diner and stiffed me because heaven forbid I was half a second late refilling their coffee cups. Before I could caution myself I was in his face fists folded.

My boys of course were cheering mommy on, no sense of danger whatsoever. I'll have to have another chat with dad about letting them watch UFC. For now though, I had this oversized jackass to cut down to size.

Hot or not, he wasn't going to get away with being a dick to my boys for just being kids. "Look here you, this is a public park if you don't want people mucking up your day then you should've stayed in your cage or wherever it is they keep your breed of species."

Uh-oh. I guess the finger in the chest was going a bit too far if the way he looked from it to me was any indication.

I had the dumb thought that he had the most amazing eyes I'd ever seen on anyone. Laurie what the hell are you doing? I took a step back when his nose flared like he was inhaling my scent and I felt heat rising up my neck to my face.

Just what had my boys landed me in this fine morning anyway?

Chapter TWO

BRETT

Is this chick for real? I could bench press her one handed and here she was flying up in my face. I ought to snap that finger in half, but that would just land me in more shit.

I towered over her and growled when she poked into me. Meanwhile her damn minions were garbling some shit, like they really thought mommy could take my ass.

"Listen lady you might wanna move it before you lose it. What the hell is your problem anyway?"

Granted, I'm not usually such an asshole, and especially not to a complete stranger of the female persuasion.

But a combination of a fucked up workweek coupled with family drama bullshit, has brought me to the end of my fucking rope.

Normally I would've cautioned her kids about approaching any large animal, in a more genteel way; but her whole attitude stunk. I guess women who looked like her thought they should get a free pass; she could kill that shit.

If Gunther sunk his teeth in one of them, she'd probably try to take me for hundreds of thousands of dollars. It would only take her finding out who I am for the dollar signs to start floating around in her head. I've seen it too many times to count.

"Listen douchebag, I don't know what climbed up your ass and died but..."

"You need to calm your little ass down lady, and watch your mouth."

We were toe to toe at this point, and I could only be grateful that there was no one else around to witness this catastrophe.

Her little terrors were sitting on the grass looking on, like they were at the circus or some shit, and guess what, my fucking traitorous dog was sitting on his haunches between them, tongue hanging, enjoying the show.

"Don't you tell me to calm down, you overgrown ape." She was really asking for it, and what the hell was she wearing...? More importantly, what the fuck was my malfunction?

You've got to be shitting me. I took a quick look down between us. Yep, my boy sure knew how to pick them, hard as a fucking pike.

Shit, at least she hadn't noticed, she was too busy railing at me, to notice that I'd stopped talking altogether.

I was too shocked by my body's reaction. Seems like everything was working against me today; first my dog and now, well, my other dog.

How the hell was I going to diffuse this situation? There were a lot of gradients at work here all of a sudden.

First, my quick gander at her finger showed no sign of a wedding ring, not even the outline of one.

That didn't mean anything though in this day and age so I have to do some fishing to be sure.

This information is suddenly of great importance, because from my boy's reaction, there was a good possibility that the little dynamo was going to be under me sometime in the near future.

While she railed away at me I stood back and took her all in. Short, just like I like 'em, built up top, nice ass and gorgeous.

Her hair wasn't my usual blonde, which is a shocker. I don't remember dating anything else, not even when I was a kid.

I've always had a type; she wasn't it. So why the fuck was my dick doing the mambo over this raven haired, green-eyed sea-witch?

It was time to get to the bottom of this shit, but she was still going full steam ahead with that lip of hers.

I couldn't very well choke her to cut off her stream of invectives, so I did the next best thing. I placed my hand over her mouth. "It's done."

"Motherfucker if you don't get..." She swore as soon as I started to remove my hand so I had to put it back.

"Ssh, not in front of the kids babe." I grinned down at her just to confuse her even more. It's perverse, but for some reason I got a kick out of flustering her. I wonder if all that fire transferred to the bedroom?

She looked at me like I'd just dropped out of an unidentified flying object, good; at least she'd stopped threatening my ass with bodily harm.

When I was sure I had her attention I removed my hand again, turned to the boys and my ex dog and snapped my fingers.

"You two over here." I pointed to my vacated park bench and was only slightly surprised to see them toddle on their tiny legs to obey.

Meanwhile, their mother was looking on like a hooked fish, mouth and eyes wide open. My sidekick that I'd spent thousands of dollars feeding, sheltering, and not to mention vet bills, followed them, sitting down next to the bench as if on guard duty. Fucking dog.

When I turned back to her, I noticed she was looking at my hand in a weird way. At first I thought she was checking to see what kind of watch I wore; kinda like gauging my wealth or some shit, but nah, this was a different kind of look.

"What're you doing?" That stare was starting to freak me the fuck out. She looked up at me with a serious look and said with a straight face.

"I'm looking for that little tag thing they put on people when they let them out the crazy house for a day, because it wouldn't be fair to kick your ass if you're loony toons." She was trying to get in my face again.

"I repeat, calm your little ass down." I towered over her again, my nose damn near touching hers, our eyes boring into one another's. Damn she's gorgeous, maybe my day was looking up after all, we'll see.

I pointed my finger at her one last time before turning to her kids who were now sitting quietly on the bench.

I stood in front of the two miscreants, as I schooled them on dog etiquette; they looked up at me like I had the secrets to Candy land or some shit.

"Name." I pointed to little rascal number one.

"Gawick I's twee." He held up four fingers.

"You." I pointed to his obvious twin.

"Ditri, I's twee too." What the fuck? I turned to look at her, sure that my next words were going to rile her up again. She did seem to be a bit prickly.

"Could you maybe have given these kids some names that they could at least pronounce? And close your mouth babe, you're starting to look off."

Chapter THREE

BRETT

Oh she looked like she'd really like to do me in now, but seriously, what was with people and giving their kids fucked up names?

"That's it we're out of here, come on boys." She made to get the little imps off the bench, but she was too late.

While we were having our stare off, the two spawns of hades had ignored everything I said, and were now busy rolling around with my overpriced ex dog, that seemed to think he was a mascot or some shit.

"Why the hell are you wound so tight anyway, not getting any?" Okay, I know myself pretty well and I'm pretty sure I was antagonizing her on purpose.

Something about the way she lit up like a firecracker just got to me. Of course she started steaming and my boy was on the rise again. Not that he'd gone down much, no, he was playing peek-a-boo or some shit.

It was that shit she was wearing too, some sort of yoga thing I think they call it; fire red around the top and black down the legs.

It hugged her ass like a second skin and the little midriff top showed off a little of the skin of her tummy. She was going to fuck around and get her ass bred again messing with me.

What in the fuck? My dick just creamed pre-cum at the thought of breeding her. Maybe I'd had too much stress here lately, what the fuck was I doing?

She had two kids, was probably more trouble than she was worth, and I'm standing here in the middle of the park on a Saturday morning thinking about fucking a kid into her. I've finally cracked under the pressure.

"Are you always this rude? And keep your eyes off my ass douche." She folded her arms and glared at me, bringing me back from where the fuck I'd gone in my head.

"If you don't want men ogling your ass, don't put it on display, by the way your nipples are hard."

Her hands flew up to cover the evidence, but it was too late, the damage had already been done. It was nice to see that she was in the same predicament as I.

Her face was a red ball of fire and she looked almost vulnerable as she looked up at me. I knew if I went soft I would get nowhere with her.

So although for some fucked up reason I had the urge to wrap my arms around her and tell her everything was going to be alright I didn't.

"So, there're two ways this could end, you and I could both go our separate ways and never see each other again." Good that slight look that flashed across her face said she didn't like that idea either.

"Or, we can decide to be civil, make plans to get together again some time soon, like tonight, and see where this takes us."

She took a minute to compose herself and come up with a way to fuck with me, as if I was expecting anything different from Ms. Difficult.

"Why the hell would I want to go anywhere with you?" That mouth of hers is gonna get her in trouble, I can see it already. I wasn't accustomed to being talked to like that, and my dick was loving that shit.

"Babe it's a hundred and ten out here and your nipples look like you just left a freezer. It doesn't take a rocket scientist to figure it out. You want the goods, I'm giving you a way to get them, don't play dumb and fuck it up. Why do you women do that shit?"

"See, now I'm convinced that you're crazy, who talks to a complete stranger like that?"

"I'm not crazy sweetheart, I just call it like I see it." By now I had moved a little closer to her, all the while keeping an eye on the goings on on the ground, just in case my dog remembered what the fuck I bought him for and went on the attack.

"Oh yeah, and what do you see?" she had her hands on her hips, one leg tapping the floor and her lip curled. I could already taste the flavor of whatever she had on her lips that made them shine, probably strawberry.

I took my time looking her over, probably shouldn't have done that, now my cock was thumping in time to my heartbeats.

"I see a sexually frustrated young woman, who is hiding her obvious attraction for me behind false bravado." I was full of shit but she didn't need to know that.

My words had the desired affect and she puffed up like a rooster ready to blast me. Why the hell did I find that so adorable? She opened her mouth and I put my finger across her lips again, risking life and limb.

"Uh-uh-uh, kiddies on deck...hey Garret, Dmitri, how about some ice cream?" I kept my eyes on hers as I addressed the kids.

"Yeah ice queam." The shouts and yells were loud enough to wake the dead. Meanwhile momma was back to looking at me like she was gonna kill my ass.

"Now see what you've done you big ape."

"Not to worry ice cream's on me."

I'm not stupid; I know she was thinking of ways to shoot me down; probably a little over cautious after being burned by the asshole sperm donor.

If the way to a man's heart is his stomach, then the way to a woman's is her little darlings.

I didn't know what the fuck I was doing, or worst yet, what had gotten into me, but something was going on here.

As a man accustomed to following my gut, I couldn't just walk away. When I left my house this morning I was mad as fuck at the world, now things seem to be looking up.

It's been a while since I've been on this side of the great divide, I'm usually the one being hunted; it might be fun doing the pursuing this time.

I'm about to play this game right and see how far it takes me. Maybe Gunther was good for something after all; he'd netted me a hot young cutie. Fucking dog.

Chapter FOUR

LAURIE

I watched as he herded my kids together, and his dog, and they just walked ahead of him like nothing, huh.

I didn't stop to ask myself why I was letting this happen. I wasn't really afraid, in fact I felt completely relaxed around him, which made no sense whatsoever because my first impression had been that he was crazy.

But I do have a thing about honesty, and if he wasn't that, then he really was the craziest son of a bitch I'd ever met.

I'm not one to be swayed by good looks, though he did have those in spades. That's not the reason I was following him out of the park like a lamb to the slaughter though, no.

There was something about him that made me feel, safe. I have no idea what that was about. It could be his height, the way he seems to block everything else out when he's standing close.

It could be the way he looked at me just then when he was telling me about my ass. Like he would devour me if we were alone.

I don't think anyone has ever looked at me with so much heat before, it made me feel just a little weak, which is probably not such a good thing. Once bitten twice shy, doesn't seem to hold up too well under his brand of hotness.

When we reached the ice cream-parlor, which was just a little ways outside of the park, he tied his dog and bent at the knee and spoke, like he expected the animal to understand what he was saying. Then again, the way Gunther turned his head to the side and watched him, maybe he did.

He hadn't said one word to me while we were walking, other than to finally exchange names; no he was very slick, he talked to the boys the whole way here and they loved it.

That was another thing, the way my boys just fell in line for him, that's a first. He'd gone from gruff and mean to friendly in the blink of an eye and my two little men were eating it up.

After opening the door for us, I was a little confused when he just walked up to the counter before asking what they wanted.

But I felt my heart give a little when he walked back towards us with a bowl with what looked like water, and went outside to his dog. After some more neck scuffing he was back.

"Okay boys time to wash our hands, lets go." Oh this was gonna be good, finally my boys will put mister big shot in his place.

Everyone knows little boys hate water, mine especially. Imagine my surprise, and yes, a little hurt, when my two traitors fell in line and walked off; with a compete stranger that I'd just met in the park.

What kind of mother are you? I hurried after them and stood right outside the door; anyone coming this way might think I'm a pervert because I had my ear pressed to the door.

"Okay Garret my man, you first; wow you really like the dirt don't you lil man, you sure you left some in the park?" I heard the water running and I don't know what was going on in there, but there were lots of giggles and then I heard Dmitri's little voice saying 'do me, do me.'

"Okay sport you're up." And they were off again; were my boys starved for male attention? My dad is basically the only one they know and he spends lots of time with them when he can, but sometimes lots of time would go by if dad's too busy.

I couldn't think about that now though, because they were coming out, but later I'll have to revisit that thought. Not that there was much I could do about it.

After the fiasco that I had made of my life, I was bound and determined to make something of myself for me and my boys, and falling into bed with every Tom Dick and Harry I meet, just to find them a father figure, wasn't part of that agenda.

They came through the door and he stopped short when he saw me. I was about to explain myself, but the look he gave me told me he understood.

"Hey look who's here." He smiled at me while once again herding the boys back into the parlor. He took us to a table in the corner, where someone had set up two high chairs; I looked at him questioningly.

"I told Melanie to get them ready for us."
"Melanie?" Why did I feel a pang of jealousy at the way he said the name?

"The lady behind the counter, I come here a lot so we're on a first name basis." I looked him up and down, because he did not look like someone who was into indulging in sweets; in fact he looked fuck hot as the saying goes.

When his mouth was closed he was actually a pretty awesome package. I guess he caught my look because he grinned at me and said.

"Gunther likes ice-cream, every once in a while I come here to get him some."

"You shouldn't give dogs ice cream."
"Who says?"
"I'm not sure, but I'm sure I've heard it before."

"Gunther likes ice cream, he gets ice cream, the fu...heck they know, are they dogs? Okay boys what'll it be, chocolate, vanilla, strawberry, or something fun?"

"Fun."
"Fun." They chortled together, clapping their hands with glee.
Are you kidding me right now? I've had to eat vanilla ice cream for the past year or so because they refused to try anything else.

So when I could afford to buy it at the grocery store, it was usually a generic brand of vanilla. I could only look on with my mouth hanging open, as he walked them to the counter to pick out something 'fun'.

After they'd noisily made their choices, he brought them back and helped me put them in their chairs, before turning back to me.

"And you, what do you like?"
I wanted to fold my arms and pout like a brat but I settled for a little sulk.

“I'll have Black Forest frozen yoghurt please." My voice didn’t sound too whiny but it was close.

He actually ruffled my hair and the boys' before heading off. Once again he made the trek outside to give Gunther his ice cream before coming back in.

When he brought the tray with our goodies over, I thought to myself, this guy really doesn't know anything about kids. He'd gotten them two waffle shells instead of cones.

Before I could tell him of his colossal blunder, he explained his reasoning and I had to wonder if he made it a habit of picking up strange women with children, because he seemed to know way too much.

"I figured with a cone they'd spill more of it than they actually get into their mouths, this way they get the best of both worlds, they have their ice cream and their cone."

"Eat up boys." He gave the order and my little piglets went to town. I watched and listened as this guy, who now that I wasn't blinded by fury looked like something from a GQ magazine, cleaned my sons' faces and chatted with them.

What the hell? I was more than a little jealous too, so I decided to interject and countermand him. Of course he saw right through me.

"Don't be jealous little mama, it's good that they get to know me, since they're going to be seeing a lot of me from now on."

"What?" Was he serious? I think Mr. Hottie was stark, raving nuts. It's a pity too, with that wild mane of dark hair and those piercing blue eyes, not to mention dimples; he could've been a real catch.

"It's short notice now, but in a couple weeks, after you've gotten to know me better, my mom would love to babysit while we go out. But for now I'm sure you have someone you call on when you need to be somewhere."

He looked at me expectantly and I felt that slight tremble in my limbs at the way those eyes of his seemed to be undressing me.

I swallowed the saliva that was starting to pool in my mouth and tried for a cool attitude once I did answer him, and not like a love sick teenager with a crush.

"Hah, somewhere like where? At the end of the day, after I've finished running around behind these two, I'm lucky if I can still put one foot in front of the other. And to answer your question, my dad's the only one I trust with them and he's working the late shift tonight, sorry."

"No problem, I'll bring dinner to you, what does the boys like to eat?" He helped Garret spoon some sprinkle-covered ice cream into his mouth before wiping off his chin.

Okay this guy is probably an axe murderer or something. What guy that looked like that, would go out of his way to be with a woman with not one but two kids? Still I found myself answering him.

"They like pizza."
"Okay boys, pizza for dinner okay with you?"
"Wait a min..."

Their loud chorus of 'pisa pisa' was answer enough I guess, but now I was left with doubts, something just wasn't adding up here.

"You know, most guys would run hard in the opposite direction from a young mother with kids, why are you trying so hard?"

He studied me for a good minute, in which time I begun to squirm in my seat. The guy really knows how to do it with a look, but why bother? He gave me this sly grin like he knew exactly what I was thinking, before leaning over to whisper in my ear.

"Have you seen your ass Laurie? It's a thing of beauty, I can't wait to get my hands along with other things on it." He sat back with a smirk, not even caring that my panties were now destroyed.

I'll need to have a talk with my ovaries later; I think they were doing handsprings or something.

Meanwhile he just sat back like he hadn't just sent me into a tailspin. It had been a long time since I'd given any thought to the horizontal mambo, four years to be exact, but I sure was giving it a lot of thought this morning.

I watched him covertly as he interacted with the boys. As a mom I can spot a fake a mile away.

It takes a lot to put up with somebody else's kids, especially when they were as rambunctious as my boys, but he held his own.

It didn't seem to faze him when they got ice cream all over themselves and the table, though I cringed as I waited for the complaining to start.

But he never uttered a word, just kept right on talking to them as if he understood every word, while we took turns wiping their little faces after each mishap.

By the time we were done, and the boys were cleaned up again, I was halfway to hopeful.

I kept holding my breath waiting for the letdown, but none came and my boys seemed to be completely taken in.

Was I making a mistake here, letting them get that close to him? He was a complete stranger after all. Maybe it was a bit late to be putting on the brakes, but shouldn't I do something? I was so lost.

Now I know what the other single mothers I met with at Gymboree were talking about. It really is hard to know what's the right thing to do in a situation like this.

If it were just me I probably wouldn't think twice, but was it really safe to get my boys involved?

He didn't give me much of a choice when it was time to leave for home. Once again he took the reigns and led the way.

I have to admit it felt really good letting someone else take the lead for a change. It had been quite sometime since that had been the case.

He did it so casually too, like he dealt with kids everyday. "Oh shit, you're not married are you?" I'm such an idiot; of course that's it.

"That excuse isn't gonna work for you babe, I'm free and single...for the time being." He actually looked around me at my ass while holding both boys by the hand.

Oh man, I wonder if they make panties out of some kind of waterproof material. And where does he get off dong this to me with just a look?

He knew it too the infuriating man, because my nipples were sticking out again and his eyes were right there.

His boyish grin didn't fool me for one second, and I had the fleeting thought that maybe I should look into some kind of birth control.

Just to be safe mind you, I had no plans on jumping into bed with him no matter how weak in the knees he makes me.

"Stop worrying that pretty little head of yours, I can see the wheels turning. We're just going to take things nice and slow until you get your bearings, and then we'll do things my way."

"That's what I'm worried about." If he moved this fast with everything, who knows how long before we ended up in bed together. Somehow I don't think I could hold him off for much longer than he was willing to give me.

My boys are known for getting me into situations, it looks like this time they'd really landed mommy in a pickle.

Chapter FIVE

BRETT

I walked them home afterwards for two reasons, one, I needed to know where she lived, and quite frankly I didn't trust her to tell me the truth, and two, she needed help with the two pre convicts. They sure were a handful.

They fought each other for my shoulders as I took turns carrying them and I knew that I had won them over at least, now I just had to work on mom.

She kept giving me looks when she thought I wasn't paying attention, but unbeknownst to her, I was becoming very aware of her every move.

There was something in her that pulled at me, I haven't figured it out yet, but I promised myself that I would get to the bottom of it before long.

I knew as a thinking man that if I get involved with a woman with kids it was going to be about more than the bedroom.

Which means in all good conscience I can't take this thing any farther unless I was really interested in more than a quick fuck.

I can't say that I had a handle on exactly what was going on, but I know it felt different from every other experience I'd had in the past.

I wasn't already planning my escape route in my head, which is something I've been doing when it comes to the opposite sex, since I was old enough to date.

I always went into a relationship expecting it to end, don't ask me where I got that fucked up mentality, my parents have been married for fucking ever and so are my grandparents.

But I've always had a very cynical view of matrimony. Now I find myself contemplating things that no rational man in his right mind would be, after only just meeting someone and still not knowing the first thing about them.

The boys kept me too busy to think too deeply with their antics though, and I wondered how the hell someone as tiny as she was could keep up with them.

I don't know why, but I look at the three of them and my heart does funny things in my chest. It's not just her then, it's the whole fucking package and instead of running hard in the other direction like she'd said earlier, I find myself wanting to immerse myself in them.

I told the boys a story as we walked to avoid any more of their theatrics.

"We're here." Her voice, which was suddenly sounding unsure and shy, broke into my story of pirates on the high seas, which they had been enjoying.

I didn't like their neighborhood, the houses were too close and they were all a little worn. But I knew if I said anything, my little prickly pear would have my ass.

I had to smile at that, after being accustomed to everyone bending over backwards to kiss my ass, it was surprisingly refreshing to meet someone who gave it to me straight.

Thinking of that shit just brought my drama back to the forefront, but somehow it no longer had the same affect.

It felt as though meeting her and the boys had helped to smooth out the rough edges, which was too strange for words, considering our meeting.

"So I'll be back at about six with pizza, that about right, or do the boys eat earlier?" She looked a little embarrassed by the question.

"Um, they usually eat around five thirty but you don't have to..."

"Uh-uh-uh, none of that. Five-thirty it is, Laurie relax. I have a mom who's a mama bear, I know how moms are about their kids, so I know if I want you, you come with kids.

It's not a problem for me, I'm not a total dick." I made sure four little ears were occupied and hadn't heard me.

While the boys were busy turning my attack dog into a bitch, I pulled her into me and laid one on her.

Shit, I miscalculated there, she was sweet and soft, and her ass felt amazing when my hands passed over it slightly.

The taste of her went right to my head and places south, and if I hadn't known I was in serious trouble before, I knew it now.

She kissed me like she was starved for it, and the way she clung to me did strange things to my heart. I actually felt that shit shift in my chest. Scared the fuck out of me.

I pulled back and studied her, trying to see what it was about her. She still had her eyes closed with a look of pure pleasure on her face, and then she bit into her lip and sighed and my cock jumped.

Fuck, I'm so gone. What the fuck? All I did was go for a run. This woman needed to come with a warning sign. How the fuck could life just throw you a curve ball without any warning like that?

From sitting on a park bench minding my own business, to falling for a mouthy little sexpot with obvious baggage.

Anyone who knew me knew I wasn't the baggage type. Usually I'd be headed hard in the opposite direction, with her I was more than ready to jump right in with both feet.

I knew my personality wouldn't let me back down from this. I'm going to have to see this through to whatever conclusion was in the cards for us.

As I looked at the boys who were looking back and forth between their mom and me like 'what the fuck dude', I couldn't help wondering if I was looking at my family.

When she finally opened her eyes and looked at me, I smiled weakly at her, what else could I do? She'd just fucked up my well-organized life and I hadn't even fucked her yet.

"Okay boys go with mom." I snapped my fingers and my worthless ass dog came to my side as she headed up the broken steps with the boys.

First thing I have to do is get them the fuck outta there, fast moving yeah, but what the fuck, life's too short to play around, and waiting for something I wanted has never been my strong suit anyway.

I watched until they were safely inside, after she'd made the boys thank me for the one-hundredth time. Halfway down the block I called Candice Cantone.

"Mom, I just met your future daughter in law." Yeah I said those words, on a Saturday morning while walking down a street littered with little shops, and little white haired old women pushing their little pushcarts up and down the sidewalk, on their way to and from the market.

She screamed so loud I had to take the phone away from my ear with a grin. Of course she wanted to know everything, so I filled her in.

Not surprisingly, she wanted to know how soon she could get her hands on the boys, but I cautioned her to let me work my magic first. The woman is a baby hog.

She didn't question my certainty either, if there's anyone who knows me in this world it's my mom.

She'd been having a hard time dealing with the drama that had been unfolding in my life here lately, that's why I didn't want to wait to share my good news with her. We could both do with some positive news right about now.

I was a mess for the next few hours before it was time to go back to them. I kept replaying everything about the morning over and over in my head. I don't remember ever being that hung up on a woman before.

Shit, I didn't even know her last name, didn't know who she was, where she came from. None of that seemed to matter though, because my dick was already in a twist.

Looks like my two dogs were running the show. I needed to learn more about the sperm donor though, make sure he was out of the picture.

I'm not into sharing, and I damn sure wasn't about to have some other dick sniffing around her once I claimed her.

I hope like hell the coast was clear, she didn't strike me as the type to accept my dinner offer if she was involved though; and the way she'd kissed me said she was starved. If her pussy was as sweet as her mouth my cock was going to be very happy with me.

At about five I called my favorite pizza place and gave them her address, before heading out to her place. I decided to take the hummer. Maybe before bedtime we could take the boys for a ride, and I figured they'd get a kick out of it.

I actually rushed over there like a teenager on his first date. I stopped and got her some flowers. I had no idea what her favorites were, so I got them to make me up a bunch with some of everything, which made the thieving ass florist very happy.

"Damn, shoulda got her some chocolate and maybe some dessert for the boys." It was too late now though, and I was sure there were no luxury chocolatiers in this neighborhood. I have to work on getting her out of here, but I'm gonna need more info before I make that move.

Some women take that independent shit too far and fuck shit up for no good reason. I'm hoping she's not one of those, because I would hate for us to butt heads over something this important so early in our relationship.

She answered the door looking all flustered and cute. Her hair was all over the place, but she'd obviously changed and was now wearing low-rise jeans and a cute camisole top, which my boy seemed to appreciate.

But something told me she could be wearing a gunnysack and he would still stand up and take notice.

"Come on in if you dare it's a madhouse in here." I satisfied myself with a quick kiss on her lips, which seemed to fluster her as much as the lip lock earlier had.

I walked past her into the tiny apartment and saw the boys on the living room floor with a mountain of toys. They squealed when they saw me and ran over babbling at me a mile a minute.

"What's up boys you being good for mommy?" I got down on the floor with them and prepared to be entertaining. Mom had given me some pointers on how to behave. As she'd put it 'if you're going to be a dad you have to start with the boys now'.

"Uh huh." They lied their asses off as they showed me their toys, sometimes holding my face to keep my attention.

She sat in a chair across from us, watching as I sat on the floor and played with building blocks. The truth is, it wasn't so bad; I would've tried for her sake, but I actually liked the little tykes.

I felt relaxed and carefree, nothing at all like I expected, maybe this daddy thing wasn't so hard after all. Who the fuck had I turned into in that park anyway?

I was never interested in kids before, not mine or anyone else's. At twenty-eight I figured I had a long ways to go before I started down that road.

Now here I am seriously contemplating giving this woman and her sons my name and I hadn't even known them twenty-four hours.

"I ordered the pizza so it should be here any minute." At the word pizza the boys went crazy and started shouting their version of the word and the blocks were soon forgotten, as Laurie got up to set the table.

"Come on boys let's go help mom."

I had her show me where everything was, and me and my new pals set the table, while she watched with an indulgent smile on her face.

"I should keep you around more often, you seem to get them to behave in ways I can't."

"That's the idea." I stole a quick kiss in passing which made her blush prettily, but I didn't make a big deal out of it, just kept going.

I planned on conditioning her to my touch. I know she was still a little skittish yet, but she had every right to be, I would've been disappointed if she wasn't. But it was my job to put her at ease.

Hopefully I can be patient long enough to let her get her bearings, but it might be close. I haven't ever had a female tie me up in such knots before, so we were both treading on virgin territory.

The pizza arrived and I helped her cut tiny pieces for the boys and get them set up in their booster seats. Again she watched me like a hawk as the boys proceeded to make a mess.

I pretended not to notice and kept up a running conversation with her. I found out she wanted to go back to school full time, but was waiting until the boys were old enough for Pre K and she'd raised enough money to do it.

She wasn't complaining about her life, but I learned by listening to her that the life of a single parent was tough.

I didn't want to bring up the ex in front of the boys, but I was dying to know. The more I listened to her, the more I wanted to know about her life.

She was smart and sassy, and so completely different from everything I was accustomed to. She was real, that's what it was, that element that I had been trying to put my finger on.

There aren't many 'real' women in my life. More like leeches and rattlesnakes, always out for whatever they can get.

I was growing tired and truth be known, jaded by the whole scene. My life so far had been gold diggers and opportunist. Even women who came from wealthy families were trying to land me because they wanted more.

But it was what they were willing to do, the lengths they were willing to go to that had finally made me want to wash my hands of all of them.

***

Pizza was a hit, if the amount of sauce all over their little faces was any measure, and I knew she didn't want to say anything, but I was pretty sure that it was bath time, so I took the initiative.

I had no qualms about trying to ingratiate myself in her and her sons' lives. In the last half an hour or however long it had taken Chaos and Mayhem to fuck the whole kitchen up with pizza sauce, I'd fallen head over heals in love with all three of them.

I didn't even whimper at the lost of my freedom, didn't stop to think about what the fuck I was getting myself into. As far as I'm concerned, I'd already made up my mind, and now all that was left to do, was to get her on board.

"So how do we do this? Do we throw them in a pool or something until they're all cleaned up?"

She looked at me like I was crazy and it was hard keeping the laughter inside, until she caught on that I was messing with her.

"I'm sure they'd love that but there's no pool."

"Fine then, why don't you start on this mess and I'll get them started in the tub. Or maybe I should just take them outside and hose them off." I picked Garret up and held him away from me with his sauce covered everything.

Of course if I did it to one I had to do it to the other to avoid a screaming match.

We ended up sharing bath duty, which was pretty simple. She just put them in the tub with some toys and sat there talking to them while we watched, until it was time to wash their hair and their little bodies.

I was the main attraction after that it seemed, each of them found a million things to show me, until they grew a little tired and fussy and it was time to take them out.

Again she grew embarrassed by their behavior, and I wondered who the hell she'd been dealing with that she kept doing that shit.

"Hey how about taking the boys for a spin in my truck? That always used to work on me and my brothers according to mom."

I could see from her face that she was a little skeptical and I had to throttle back.

What a dick; you just met her and her kids, invited yourself to her home, which now come to think of it was a minor miracle that she'd let me in, and now you wanted her to get into your vehicle with you at night. What an ass.

I had a hunch and went with it. "You said your dad usually watched the boys, does he know I'm here?" She blushed and tried to hide behind her hair.

"Smart baby, real smart." By now we were getting the boys into their pajamas and I was amazed at how right this shit felt, being here with them like this.

"Give me your phone, was he the last number you called?" She nodded her head and looked at me skeptically. I pressed redial on the last number in the log and waited while it rang.

A gruff voice came over the phone. "Well child of mine, I see you're still alive so the hottie from the park didn't kill you over pizza."

"Uh, this is the hottie from the park." I thought she would fall through the floor at that.

"Hey son how's it hanging? So you survived the tornadoes two huh!"

"Looks like; listen I just suggested taking them for a spin before bedtime, but I think your daughter is thinking serial killer, so I thought maybe I'd call you and give you the particulars, this way she'd be more comfortable."

"Give her the phone son." I passed the phone to the still embarrassed Laurie.

"Hey dad thanks for embarrassing me." She wouldn't even look at me, meanwhile my soon to be sons were trying to climb me.

"Anytime kiddo, now tell the nice man to give you his ID." I could hear him through the phone, so I reached into my back pocket, handed it over, and waited while she gave him the info.

"Ho-ho-ho, well he doesn't have a record." He was clicking away on keys in the background and I remembered she'd said he was a cop.

"If he doesn't have a record why do you have him in the system chief?" "Well now because your boy there is a multibillionaire and we have..."

"He's a what?" She moved the phone from her ear to her chest and glared at me. "Get out of my house." She was furious and fuck if I knew why. The boys reacted to the sudden stress in her voice so I took the phone from her.

"Thanks chief I'll take it from here, we good?" I accepted the other man's approval before hanging up the phone; next I turned to the boys.

"You two stay here, mommy and I will be right back." I grabbed her arm and pulled her from their room. Pushing her back against the wall in the hallway, I looked down at her.

"Explain."
"What am I, a lost bet or something? Why else would a billionaire be slumming with a single mom and her kids?"

Her face was like a storm cloud, but the thing that really got me was the hurt that was in her eyes. I took my time and got my words together so that I didn't fuck this up.

I'm not too much into rash movements, but as a businessman I know a good deal when I see one, and everything that I believe in told me this was one of those times.

I just had to get past the first day and it should be a cinch, so here goes.

"Do you remember what I told you in the ice cream parlor babe? It's your ass, I can't wait to get my hands, my cock, and anything else in it, on it, over it, along with some other body parts of yours."

I pressed my hard cock into her, "You feel that? That feels like a lost bet...fuck me..." I became tongue tied and lost all train of thought because I'm not sure what happened just then.

Maybe I pressed into her clit just right or something, but the hot little number was cumming on my cock. No joke.

I pressed harder and watched in amazement as she shook and her breathing sped up while she made use of the hard cock that was pressing into her through her clothes.

I wrapped one hand in her hair and pulled her hip forward with the other as I took her mouth in a deep tongue-thrusting kiss.

I lifted her so that her legs wrapped around me as I sucked her tongue hard and ground my cock into her.

My heart was doing cartwheels in my chest and I was pretty sure there was going to be a wet spot in the front of my jeans any minute now.

My hand went down between us and I felt her heat just before I reached for my zipper. All I could think about was getting inside all that wet heat.

Fuck, you can't take her here Brett, the boys... No sooner had I had the thought than they came toddling out of the room barraging me with their variation of 'what're you doing?'

I pressed my forehead against hers, "Fuck Laurie you just sealed your fate." I kissed her forehead and squeezed her hip before pulling away a little bit and letting her legs drop from around me.

I couldn't let her go all the way though, not just yet. So I kept her pinned to the wall.

After I'd caught my breath and was sure that I could speak coherently I turned to the boys.

"We're just playing a game boys. Say, how would you like to go for a ride in my tank?"

"Yeah." They chorused together even though I knew they had no idea what I was talking about. I was just buying some time for their mother who was flushed and seemed to me like she was still having aftershocks.

Fuck, if she goes off like that from over the clothes contact, what would she feel like wrapped around my cock?

Better think of something else Cantone you're not in much better shape yourself. I had three sets of eyes on me. Two wide-eyed and curious, and the third, a little wide eyed but I think her curiosity stemmed from someplace else.

"You good here baby?" I tapped her hip because she was still not saying anything, and that seemed to snap her out of it.

"Yeah I'm fine." She straightened her clothes and fixed her hair, which I don't remember mussing, and I couldn't resist one last peck.

"I'll be right back, make sure the boys are dressed warm enough okay." I left her as she was rounding them up.

I went downstairs to get their car seats situated, and to give myself a chance to cool down, before running back up to get the three of them.

She was a little better, or I should say she no longer looked like she needed a good hard fuck, but there was no way I was going to get that picture out of my head anytime soon.

"Let's go babe, we'll take the boys for a little ride before bedtime." She refused to look at me, her face was red, and she kept fidgeting and biting her lip.

I didn't bother telling her there was no need to be embarrassed. I just got the boys strapped in while they babbled away at me.

Then I lifted her tiny ass into my truck, and of course I rubbed my semi hard cock against her again. Maybe that had been a fluke back there, maybe she wasn't as responsive as her reaction suggested.

She drew in a deep breath and I felt her body tremble. Fuck me she's for real. I couldn't help kissing her again right there out in the open.

I barely restrained myself from going too far and thought to myself that at this rate I'd better set down the ground rules fast.

I sat her in the passenger seat and stood between her thighs, making sure to keep that connection, while my mouth devoured hers. When the boys started chortling and clapping their hands I came back to my senses.

"I can't wait to get inside you, don't make me wait too long." I whispered those incendiary words in her ear, before turning her around and buckling her in, then walking around to the driver's side.

I did a little adjusting on my way around to the front of the truck and tried to get my breathing under control.

She packed a serious punch in that little body of hers, and I was right. She tasted like strawberries and hot summer sin. Where the fuck had that come from?

"Okay boys you ready?" I looked back at them after climbing behind the wheel. They babbled their versions of ready, and I took off slowly.

I'd only planned a little trip around the block, but I felt so good all of a sudden, I headed for the lake area outside of town.

It would mean at least an hour drive, but I think the boys would enjoy it, and it would give me more time with their mother.

It didn't escape my notice that she hadn't said anything since our first kiss. I wasn't sure if she was processing shit or thinking up ways to shoot me down. Good luck with that. There is no way I'm letting her get away from me now.

Reaching over the console, I took her hand in mine, rubbing my thumb over her fingers. "Talk to me babe." I kept my voice low so as not to alert the boys, who were busy speaking their secret language to each other.

At least that's what it sounded like they were doing. "Um..." She lifted her free hand and dropped it back in her lap, all the while biting into that bottom lip.

"Laurie, word of warning. I'm barely hanging onto my control and only because of the boys, but you keep biting into your lip like that and I will take you."

She released her lip and looked at me like she was afraid I was going to make good on my threat right then and there.

"Not to worry babe, I said if the boys weren't here, but they are so you're safe, just don't do that anymore okay, it has a weird effect on my dick."

I wanted to ask her if she reacted that way to all men, like maybe the sperm donor. The thought made me very...not happy. Fuck it.

"Do you always react like that to stimuli?" Back to the lip biting again. "I don't know, I've only been with one guy and it was only once."

"You..." I pulled off onto the side of the road and stared at her. "You've only had sex once in your life?"

She nodded with her cheeks inflamed. What I was about to do would either scare the shit out of her or...I don't know what the fuck.

"That's it, I'm going to be the next and only other guy to have you. Do whatever you have to do to get that settled in your head. Today is the day you met the man you're going to spend the rest of your life with."

I could see I'd blindsided her with that one, but I was surprising myself as well so that was okay. There was just something about her and the boys, the whole package. And I already had the dog, readymade family if you ask me.

To think, that my first impression of her had been less than flattering. Spending time with her has shown me that she is a whole lot more than I'd given her credit for.

She's one of those females that make a man think of hearth and home. Of protecting his woman from the big bad world and keeping her safe.

The boys were an added bonus, something I would never have thought in a million years that I would go for, another man's kids.

I'd wondered about stuff like that before. A man taking on another man's family, and though I can't say that it was my ideal situation, this one worked for me, she worked for me.

She hadn't said anything as yet to my bold statement but I could see her gearing up for it, and knowing her, I might have my work cut out for me.

"We just met, what makes you think it will work? I have two kids remember? And besides, I'm nowhere near your league."

"Babe what you've got is worth a helluva lot more than I could ever afford. Don't stress it, we don't have to rush into anything...no scratch that.

I want you on a flat surface as soon as possible, but I'll give you time to see that I'm on the up and up. Not too much though, and I'm definitely not giving you that much time to think about the sex thing. That, we have got to get to like soon."

I could already imagine it in my head. Her beneath me as I pounded away at her sweet body, damn.

I can’t remember the last time a woman had tied me up in knots. In fact, I don’t think that shit had ever happened before in my life.

"I just met you Brett, I'm not exactly in the habit of jumping into bed with guys I just met." I do love that little prim and proper thing she does whenever she thinks I’m stepping over the line.

"Good for you, but this, this is different. You want to get married first?" yeah I said that shit, and I meant it too. Though I knew that she would never go for it.

I think I was dealing with another first here; a woman that I had to chase for a change. Usually I am the one being hunted, but this might be good.

I could see that my little bombshell had left her speechless, and I was growing to like this way I had of shocking her into silence.

From this morning's theatrics I knew that it was only a matter of time before she was back on her game and I was going to have my work cut out for me, so I was going to keep her off balance as much as I could for now, while I had the upper hand.

"Are you insane? We just met this morning."

"Babe." I had to lower my voice again because the two in the back were through speaking in code and were now more interested in what was going on in the front seats.

"You came on my cock when I barely touched you outside your clothes. If I hadn't stopped just now you would've done it again. I don't know how it is for women, but as a man let me tell you I am not willing to give that shit up.

Now I'm willing to give you a window of time to work shit out in your head. You've got the boys to think about after all, but make no mistake we're doing this."

I figured with her I was going to need less talk and more action. She'd already asked me if she was a lost bet so I had an idea of where her head was at.

There was obviously a truckload of things we needed to learn about each other, but I was pretty satisfied that I had all the basics.

She wasn't as crazy as I'd first thought and even if she was I'm afraid I would've still gone for it. It's not everyday a man meets a woman who has such a strong reaction to him physically.

It might not be the best thing to base a relationship on, but it was a fuck of a start.

After the week from hell, it looked like I was finally about to catch a break, three of them to be exact.

No one who knew me would recognize me. I'm the guy who likes to think things through, sometimes to death as I've been accused of often enough in the past.

I can't explain it, but this feels right. And besides, my dog already gave his stamp of approval, and I trust his judgment more than I do a lot of my two legged friends'.

She seemed to be giving some thought to my words and I was grateful that she hadn't just scoffed at what I'd said. Knowing her though, I knew it wasn't going to be that easy.

It didn't matter though; my mind was made up. I took a look at my future in the rearview mirror and smiled.

When I woke up this morning, sore at the world and not too happy with life, I had no idea I was going to meet my destiny on a park bench. Life truly is strange sometimes.

“How’re we doing back there champs?” They chortled at me and pointed out the windows babbling all the way. At least I was making headway with the boys, and I was going to keep on doing it too, until I got her just where I wanted her.

I didn’t prove myself to dad in the business world, and earn my stripes and a corner office early, by being soft.

Grandpa had taught me from a young age, ‘know your opponent son, and always go for the jugular.’ I figure this was the biggest merger and acquisition I’d ever gone after, I could do no less than my best.

Chapter SIX

LAURIE

Either I'd fallen down the rabbit hole, or I'd got myself mixed up with a nut. Who the hell thinks like that?

It was true that he made my heart race in a way that it never had, not even in my one disastrous try at romance, and I'd thought I was in love with that ass.

But I can't trust this, any of it. Things like this only happen in cheesy made for TV movies, and he's loaded on top of everything else.

That alone made my stomach hurt. I am so not the type of girl that a hot multi-billionaire would go for, especially not with my baggage. So something else had to be at play here, I just haven't put my finger on it yet.

But he seems so genuine, so sincere, and the boys already like him, not to mention what he makes me feel when he touches me.

But I can't give into this I have to be responsible. Maybe if I'd met him before. No, I can't start thinking like that either. Next thing you know I'd be resenting my boys and I will never be guilty of that.

"I can see that mind of yours working overtime over there, that's okay. Go ahead and work this shit out in your head, but don't forget what I said.

No matter where you go in your head, we're doing this, the sooner the better. Those two back there need a dad and I'm the man for the job."

"Brett be serous now, is this some kind of joke? I mean you seem too old for college pranks, so what exactly is going on here?" He looked back at the boys who were finally winding down.

"Let's get them home and settled, this conversation needs to be away from prying eyes and ears." He made a U-turn and headed back in the opposite direction.

I was on pins and needles wondering what he was going to come up with next. I could barely keep up. He seemed to have only one speed, which I should be used to by now after running around behind the boys for the past couple of years.

But this speed was entirely different, there was a lot more at stake here than a scraped knee from a fall.

I have no experience with men, my one failed attempt at a relationship had ended with me being pregnant at a young age and left holding the bag.

After the fear and self-loathing had passed in about month seven of my pregnancy, I had sat down at worked out the rest of my life.

By then I had already learned that I was expecting not one but two kids and that my life was forever changed.

Adoption was never an option, as hard as I knew things were going to be, I couldn't bear a part of me living somewhere else in the world never knowing that I existed.

This, what was going on here, was not part of my plan, no. My plan consisted of me working hard for the next few years and socking away as much as I could so that when the boys were in school, I could go back myself.

That's why we lived in the not so nice part of town and bought store brand everything. The restaurant did pretty good business and my tips were enough.

That's why I put up with the crap from the day supervisor. I always kept my goals in front of me, so that way, no matter how hard the day might be, I knew that I was one step closer to a better life.

I checked on my boys to see what they were up to. I have to admit he did have a way with my monsters, but that in no way meant he was right for me.

And that other thing, that was just a fluke, just me being hard up I guess. Those two things together were not enough for people to be making or accepting marriage proposals.

I snuck a look at him out the corner of my eye. He looked normal enough; in fact he wasn't even breaking a sweat after asking a complete stranger to marry him.

Maybe this was just something he did, one of those playboy types that you see on true crime shows, a serial dater, or worst yet, a bigamist.

None of that fit though, but I was still sure there had to be something else going on here other than what he was trying to sell me.

I can understand a guy trying to get into my pants, but I couldn't seriously believe that anyone would be willing to take on my boys and me, and especially not after just one day.

But what if he was being truthful, as farfetched as it seemed? And what if he wasn't?

I was afraid to believe or hope that anything could possibly come of it. We'll go back to the apartment and he'll probably try to get me into bed.

As soon as I turn him down he'll be gone and that will be the end of it. I'm almost tempted to go to bed with him just to get it over and done with, but I knew I wouldn't do it.

My only real regret was that the boys would miss out. They genuinely seem to like him and he's the first guy I'd ever allowed to get this close to them.

Was it only this morning that we met? Why couldn't life be simpler? Why did people have to play so many games, so that you doubted everything and everyone?

I was nineteen years old, almost twenty and my life felt like it was almost over. My choices were limited now and that's the truth.

It's something I've come to terms with a long time ago, but today, for the first time, I wish I were the type to take chances, because Brett Cantone makes me want to risk it all.

I looked back at my boys who were all but nodding off in their car seats, their little faces happy and excited because they'd had a good day, and most of it was because of this man.

My heart squeezed when I thought that I might never see him again. That if it was all just a game, no matter how much I tell myself that I'm not interested, it was going to hurt like hell.

No, I can't risk it; there was no point in setting myself up for disappointment. Jonathan had done a number on me, but I was a hundred percent sure that this one would destroy me.

***

BRETT

I know exactly what she's thinking but she has no idea who she's dealing with. Her last...whatever the fuck he was was a boy.

No boy can know what to do with a woman like her, a woman who went off like a firecracker at the feel of a man's cock.

Shit, no wonder the little fuck had ran scared. She was all woman and she had no idea what that meant to a real man.

Lucky for me I'd been in the right place at the right time. I have to remember to get my dog some Grade A steaks for the next week at least. He did good.

I pulled up outside her building and went around back to get my boys. "You get the door honey I'll bring them in."

I saw her stop short at the honey but pretended I didn't see shit. That's my plan; bombard her with the sweetness. By the time I was through, she wouldn't know what hit her and we'd be hitched.

I'm not the waiting type, never waited for a damn thing in my life. I figure she had about two weeks tops before she was under me one way or the other and that was pushing it. By then I'd probably be ready to hump a fucking knot in the floor.

I followed behind her with the boys, my eyes glued to the sway of her ass. Oh yeah, she was so getting bred; mom was going to be knee deep in grandkids in about another year or so.

She showed me to the boys' room and helped me get their shoes and stuff off before putting their pajamas on. They barely made a peep as they rolled over and went to sleep.

She had no idea just how close she was to danger as she sat there looking all motherly; and why the fuck I should suddenly find that shit sexy as fuck, who knows?

I looked around the room as she ran a hand over each boy's head, still humming the lullaby that had sent them to sleep.

I'm gonna have to do something about their beds, they looked kinda old. But again, I was sure that if I mentioned it she'd freak, so I'd just buy new ones and bring them over. Seems to me like that's the only way to deal with Ms. Laurie.

I grabbed her hand and pulled her out of the room behind me after we both kissed their little heads goodnight. I headed for the living room, a man on a mission. "Sit."

I sat her on the couch and paced back and forth, trying to get my words straight. I didn't want to scare the shit out of her, but straight forward is the only way I know.

"Listen Laurie, I don't know your whole life story, but what I do know so far I want. I want you and the boys and about six other little fuckers running around here...well not here but you get my meaning.

I don't care that we just met, that's not how I work. I go with my gut, always have and it hasn't steered me wrong yet.

Do you know what I was doing this morning while you were yelling at me?" She shook her head as her eyes followed me around the room like she expected me to pounce any minute.

"I was trying to figure out a way to fuck you in that park without our boys catching on." She almost choked.

"That's right, my cock was hard as fuck and he wanted in. Now I understand you have hang-ups, but two things. I'm not paying the price for some other asshole's fuckups, and I'm not letting you waste any more time on that shit.

That shit you had going on, hiding yourself away from life, hiding behind the boys, that died when you met me."

"This is crazy Brett, how do you expect me to feel about this? This is too much, you're too much..."

"Yeah well next time be careful whose dog your kids choose to fuck with. You got me and you're stuck. You got two weeks starting now, look at your watch, look at it."

She looked down at her wrist no doubt humoring the crazy man in her living room.

“Two weeks to the fucking hour I'm inside you." I pulled her up from the couch and kissed the fuck out of her with my hands on her tight ass, pressing my cock into her.

She groaned and I almost came, fuck. "Fuck if I'm giving that up." I let her go and headed for the door. I'd said all there was to say, let her work that shit out in her head. "Tell the boys I'll be by sometime tomorrow to see them."

I left before she could say anything else. I wanted to end the night on that note. With her looking mussed from my hands in her hair and her lips swollen from my kiss.

***

I wanted to call her as soon as I got in the house, but I refrained. I'd given her a lot to think about, and if I know my girl which believe it or not I think I do, she'll be up all night worrying.

I wish I could spare her that. It can't be easy trying to figure out what's real and what's not. Especially when there was so much at stake, so much responsibility on those little shoulders.

I can't believe I was getting this excited about taking on a readymade family. There was no hesitance in me at all, no doubt, no fear. Well not on my part anyway.

I tried to put myself in her shoes, tried to imagine what arguments she could have against us going for it, and all I could see was the time thing.

People put lots of stock in days and months and years. Not to mention the fact that we didn't exactly meet under friendly terms.

I put that aside for now though. If there was one thing I'd learned from what little exposure we'd had to each other, it was that I needed to take charge. It was the only way to get under her radar and all those defenses she had put up around her and the boys.

I wasn't even going to look too closely at my own feelings of surety. I'm not such a fuck that I would go after a young mother with two kids if I wasn't planning on sticking around, because as much as I was beginning to feel for her, I was already halfway in love with her kids.

My mind turned to the sperm donor. I hadn't asked her about him tonight, because I didn't want him to be a part of our first date, but tomorrow I'll bring it up.

It was obvious that he wasn't part of their lives, I hadn't seen any evidence of a man in her place, but where and who was he? I don't like surprises I like to know everything that I'm dealing with. And I was fucked if I was going to be jealous of some faceless fuck.

As soon as I have a name I'll start looking to see what's what. I could go around her and take care of that shit, but I didn't want us to start off on the wrong foot.

Though I was tempted to put my people on it. I'm sure I could have everything I needed by morning, but I'll try doing shit the gentlemanly way first. If I didn't like what I heard or she wasn't forthcoming, well then I'd go ahead and make an end run around her.

My phone rang and brought me back, to the here and now. That reminds me, I hadn't given her my number.

"Hello."
"Mr. Cantone, this is Pete, we've taken care of that issue for you."
"Good was it any trouble?"
"No sir, it was just as you said. She had everything hidden away in that safety deposit box. The cops have it per your orders and should be rounding her up any minute now."

"Thanks a lot Pete, good job. I'll see you on Monday then."
"Sure boss, goodnight."
"Night Pete."

I hung up the phone feeling ten pounds lighter. It's weird, but I hadn't given my latest troubles a second thought since meeting my new family.

Something that had consumed me for the better part of a month, had just drifted into insignificance when I met her, them.

That can only be a good thing right? A man with my load needs that kind of calming influence in his life; that shit is worth ten therapists.

It was still early, but I didn't feel like doing anything. I wonder what she's doing right this minute, but that wasn't so hard to guess.

No doubt she was giving thought to everything I'd thrown at her tonight, at least I hope she was.

I almost panicked when I remembered that I had no way of contacting her, but then I calmed myself. I'll just go by there first thing in the morning before she could go anywhere. I'll take breakfast, yeah, that's it.

With that thought settled firmly in my mind I flipped on the tube for some background noise. I had a lot of planning to do myself. Like finding a house for us, my apartment although it had room, was no place to raise a family.

I wonder if my Laurie ever dreamed of a white knight coming to save her. I'm sure she would prefer something better for the boys, but my conscience pricked me at the thought of using that as an argument.

Did I really want to use her kids to get my way? It seemed a bit devious now that I think about it, but I know me and if that's the only recourse opened to me then so be it.

I laid my head back against the couch and closed my eyes, reliving the day spent with them.

I can't recall the last time I'd had that much fun, and I couldn't wait for more.

I imagined all the places I wanted to take her and the boys, all the things I wanted to show them, share with them.

I had to keep cautioning myself to go slow, even in my thoughts. If it were up to me I'd have her moved in by next week or however long it took me to find a suitable home.

Speaking of which, there was something I could do. Jumping up from the couch I headed up to my home office.

I was in serious need of a sedative, not even when I was a boy was I ever this gone over a female, yet here I am, just hours after meeting and I'm ready to throw it all in.

Booting up the computer, I started surfing for homes in the area. It was too late to call a realtor but Monday seemed too far away.

I was moving pretty fast, too fast for her I'm sure, but we'll see. I'll see which way the wind blows in the morning and go from there.

The one thing I was sure of is, no matter how we get there, she was going to be my woman, mine and no one else's.

Chapter SEVEN

LAURIE

I paced the floor all night and bit my nails down to the quick. There was too much going on inside my head for me to really get a hold on anything.

My body was on fire still, and that, more than anything, occupied my mind. I'm not going to lie to myself here alone in the darkness of my apartment.

What he was offering sounded like my every dream come true. A dad for the boys, enough stability to never have to worry about them again, and I don't mean just financially.

I always knew that the boys needed a dad. I just never gave much thought as to how to get them one.

Now here he comes along, offering us everything. No, it's too good to be true. Isn't it? But how can I be sure?

If it were just myself I have no doubt I would go for it in a heartbeat, who wouldn't? He was young, hot and what he made me feel whenever he got close cannot be overlooked.

I've never wanted anything as much as I wanted to just jump into his arms, and just let him do all those things his eyes promise.

But how can I risk it? My body and a little bit of my heart were screaming at me to go for it, but my head was a hold out. I just wasn't sure that I could make that move, no matter how much I might want to.

I called my dad when the walls started to feel like they were closing in. "Hey kiddo your guest gone already?"

"He left a while ago dad."
"Uh oh, I know that voice, tell old dad all about it."
"What?"
"Don't give me that, spill it. What did he do?"
"It's not that it's just...I don't know what to make of this guy dad.

"Why do you have to make anything of him kiddo? You're young, have some fun."
"Dad, I can't believe you're saying this to me. You better than anyone else know my situation."

"That's right, that's why I can tell you that you need to lighten up and live a little."

"But dad he's a stranger..."
"Laurie, honey, I hate to tell you this, but everyone's a stranger when you first meet, that's what dating is all about."

"Yes, I know, but, the boys."

"I thought we weren't going to use the boys as a cover anymore. Look if it'll help any, I ran this guy and he's one of the good ones, surprising for someone with his kind of money, but everything I turned up says he's a gem.

There was some kind of trouble lately with one of his employees but she was in the wrong as far as I can gather."

"I don't know dad, this all seems too good to be true and this time it's not just me."

"What does your heart say?"
"I stopped listening to that a long time ago."

"That's where you've gone wrong. You need love and companionship in your life. You're too young to be this cynical Laurie, come on.

What can go wrong huh? You have a few dates and you and the boys get to enjoy the good life for a while, unless he proves you wrong and actually stick around."

"Dad, I cannot believe I'm hearing this. You're the one who's always telling me to be careful."

"I know, but I think maybe we might've taken it a bit too far. I didn't mean for you to give up on life and be afraid to live yours.

It was your first time away from home and I wanted you and the boys to be safe, but I didn't expect you to become a corpse."

"Nice dad very nice; help me, tell me what to do." It was just like old times, running to daddy when things went wrong.

He had been there for me, even when I knew that I had disappointed him. Not once had he judged or accused. That had only made the guilt sharper.

If I screwed up again I wasn't sure how I would face him. He had raised me on his own after mom passed and had done everything right, but in the end I was still a needy little girl who went looking for love in all the wrong places.

“I already told you what I think but knowing your penchant for over thinking and stressing over every little thing, you're going to do as you please anyway.

Maybe I should call Cantone on my own and put a bug in his ear.”

“Don't you dare dad, I think I've been embarrassed enough for one day. I guess I'll talk to you tomorrow.”

"Is lover boy coming over?"
"So he says but we'll see."
"Laurie, do me a favor and just try to relax. I know it's hard for you to see it, but you're a very beautiful girl and you deserve to be happy. Please let yourself be happy, that's all I've ever wanted for you."

"I'm scared dad."
"I know hon but I'm here, you'll never know unless you take a chance. You don't have to jump in with both feet at once, just dip your toes a little until you get the lay of the land, then go from there."

"Are you sure that I won't be making a fool of myself?"
"Whatever do you mean?"

"I mean dad that he's a multi-billionaire who looks like a model or movie star. He's young and single, what would he want with me?"

"I think I resent that. I would have you know that my daughter is very beautiful, smart and kind and any man would be lucky to have her, rich or poor. Not to mention he's getting the rugrats as a bonus. I think he's getting the better end of this deal."

"Aww dad, that's so sweet. You should see them with him dad, it's like they've known him all their lives, then again it could be the dog they're after."

"There you go again, I happen to know that my grandsons have great taste and even greater instincts, trust me I know these things, I'm a cop."

We didn't stay on much longer, but I hung up feeling much better. At least I didn't feel so stupid about wanting to give it a shot.

I tossed and turned that night before sleep finally claimed me, but even in my dreams there was no escape.

He was waiting for me there, full of promises and everything I'd ever wanted, and I fell right into his arms. It was quite harmless to do it here, I could enjoy the feelings he awakened in me guilt free.

***

BRETT

I was up bright and early the next morning with a smile and a new purpose. I took my time getting ready, a nice shave with no nicks thank fuck, a hot shower, and I was ready to face the day.

Mom called just as I was heading out the door but I put her off until later. She was only calling to grill me about last night anyway.

It's funny, she never showed any interest in my dating life before, maybe because I never told her that I had found her new daughter in law; but now she seems to think I don't know how to do it right.

As I was bustling around trying to get out the door, I suddenly realized, I had no idea what her routine was on the weekend. Shit I don't even know if she works today, did I tell her I was coming by? I couldn't remember.

I knew that she worked as a waitress but she hadn't said where, and apart from that I didn't know which days she worked.

The boys were in some kind of program, and she said her dad was the only one she trusted to watch them outside of that, but did that include Sundays?

I wasn't going to get any answers standing around here so I got a move on. I didn't like not hearing her voice first thing in the morning, and I promised myself that it would be the last time.

Yes, I'd lost my mind completely during the night when I couldn't get to sleep because I missed her. If this was love it was a wonder half the population wasn't stark raving nuts.

I stopped off at a local diner and got some breakfast. By the time I pulled up to their place the sun was up. Did I forget to mention that it was a little before seven in the morning?

I knew the boys woke up at this time every morning because she'd told me, so I figured I should get there before she made any plans.

My heart was actually happy when I walked up to her door and rang the bell. I could hear the boys running around and began to grin before she spoke through the door.

"Who is it?"
"Your fiancé. I held up the bag like a peace offering when she opened the door.

"Very funny." She looked cute as fuck first thing in the morning. I want that, I want to have that everyday for the rest of my life. Mussed hair sleepy eyes, and soft lips.

I reached for her but the boys were on me before I cleared the door. I gave her a quick kiss hello and passed her the bag with the food, before grabbing a hellion beneath each arm and swinging them, sending them into fits of laughter.

"Hey boys what are we up to?" they were still in pajamas with their hair matted and their eyes bright. Their little bodies were raring to go when I sat them down at the table.

"Come on boys, oh wait, mom, are the boys all cleaned up for breakfast?" "Yeah they're good they'll brush their teeth again after."

She took out the cartons of pancakes and French toast with turkey bacon and eggs. "Wait, first things first. Where's your phone?"

"Over there on the counter why?" She pointed to the phone that was on the charger and I walked over to get it.

I added all my contact numbers to her contacts and then called my number from her phone.

"What's the house phone number?"

"I don't have a house phone I just use the cell."

"Okay cool, let's get the boys fed shall we?"
"Oh my word Brett, did you buy out the whole store, what did you buy?" she pulled the cartons out of the bags while I got the plates ready.

"I wasn't sure what everyone liked, so I bought some of everything. There's juice too and milk."

By the time she was finished unpacking there was hardly any room left on the table.

I bit my tongue before I put my foot in my mouth, but I wasn't going to be able to give her as much time as I had thought.

She needed more; they needed more than this. I'm pretty sure that there were a million other women out there who would jump at the chance of what I wanted to offer her.

But of course I would fall for the one that will give me a hard time, story of my fucking life, nothing easy.

I helped her dish for the boys and cut their food into bite size pieces while they babbled away at me. I could tell that they were excited to see me, even though their mother was playing it safe. Fuck if I'm not gonna use that shit.

"So, how was your night?"
"Fine we were fine, weren't we boys?"
"Good I'm glad to hear it. Now, what are our plans for today?"

"Nothing really, we just hang around the house on Sundays. The boys drag out all their toys and we play until lunchtime and then they get to watch one of their movies and that's about it."

"You need a backyard."
"We don't have a backyard." She took a bite of her French toast and I pretended not to hear the little snip in her voice.

So that's the way it was going to be was it? Well I wasn't about to play that game. I'd spent the better part of the night giving this shit a lot of thought and I had come up with the only solution.

"Did you think about what I said last night?"
"Not in front of the kids." I looked over to make sure they were eating and not paying attention to us.

"This concerns them too, if you're going to muck shit up, you should remember that you're mucking it up for them as well.

I know you might not want to hear this, but here is reality. We met yesterday; I took one look at you and fell hard.

If you need time to get use to that idea that's fine, it threw me for a loop too, but we're both adults and I'm sure that you have enough sense to know when someone is on the up and up.

I'm too grown to play games with you or anyone else and the only reason we're having this conversation is because of the boys.

I know you need to think of what's best for them, but what I'm saying to you is that I want to help you do that.

I can't do it if you don't give me a chance. The more time it takes you to come to a decision the more time we waste, just think about that.

Whatever you want to know to make you feel comfortable I'm willing to do. You can have your father run me, do a deep search if he hasn't already.

I already told you I'm ready to take you home to meet my mom, you'd be the first since high school, and trust me, that shit really is an honor, I don't take just anyone home to mom, before yesterday, she was my favorite girl, the only one I protected.

I'm not going to beg you; that's just not my style. But I'm not walking away from you either and I'll be damned if I'll let you play the coward. So you have a choice to make. Either you're gonna take a chance and let me take care of you and the boys.

Or you're going to fuck us all over and let the past dictate the rest of your life. I'm hoping you make the right choice, it would make things so much easier on all of us and we can move forward.

If you make me sweat I can't guarantee that I won't make you pay for it later." I grinned to let her know I was playing with her and she blushed, before turning to Garret to feed him a piece of pancake.

After breakfast it was wash up time and the boys got dressed. "Why don't we take a Sunday morning drive? It's nice out, we can drive down to the beach or wherever you'd like to go."

"The beach sounds nice; I don't go that often because the boys can't swim as yet and I'm nervous about taking them on my own now that they can move around so quickly."

"The beach it is." There was an ulterior motive of course. To get to the beach we had to go through the countryside first.

Last night when I was house hunting on the net, I had seen quite a few nice places that I intended to go by and just nonchalantly point them out to her to get her reaction.

Later I'll spring it on her. There was no reason I couldn't buy her dream house while she was deciding what she wanted to do, because there was no way I was ever letting her go. She didn't need to know that now of course.

We got the boys ready and packed a bag with everything that they could possibly need for the day.

I was amazed at how much was needed just for that one little outing, and my respect for her as a mother went up a couple of notches.

At least mom had had dad and nana and an army of servants, though she was another one of those do it yourself females, but my Laurie was doing it all on her own mostly.

She looked so young this morning, maybe because I'd caught her before she'd done anything to her face. For some reason it made me even more determined to take care of her.

If I didn't know any better I would've believed something happened in that park yesterday, something otherworldly. I've never in my life had this strong urge to cover, to protect, anyone.

I've felt protective of others before, mom, my sisters, but there has never been a time when I've felt those same emotions so strongly for someone else. And especially not coupled with the heavy dose of lust that was burning a hole in my gut.

While the boys sat on the floor waiting for us, I backed her into the wall around the corner.

"Hi." I nuzzled her cheek and nibbled her ear.
"Hi." I kissed the greeting off her lips and pulled her in close. That same inferno from the night before singed me and she reacted the same.

She was all but climbing my dick and I realized what she was doing. Adjusting our bodies, I lined up my hard cock with her pussy through the soft sweats she wore.

I could feel her better this way than through the jeans. There was a slight tremble in her limbs as I ground my cock into her, and just as she'd done the night before, she climaxed.

I gritted my teeth and held myself still until she got what she needed, but it was hard as fuck not to unzip and drive in. Her mouth was ravenous on mine as I fed her my tongue.

We both needed to come up for air and I left my face buried in her neck while she blew into my chest.

I pulled back when I was under control again and looked down at her. “You really don’t want to see where this goes? You really think that either one of us are ever going to find that with anyone else?”

She didn’t answer, but I hadn’t expected her to. “You ready to go?” I kissed her forehead and dropped my arms from around her.

“Just two minutes.” She started to head for the bathroom but I stopped her. “Don’t do anything to your face, I like it just like that.”

She blushed and nodded before escaping into the bathroom and leaving me alone with the boys, who were only too happy to have their new toy back.

Poor Gunther, I should've brought him along, but I hadn't been sure what we would be doing and this apartment was not big enough for him to just hang out in.

We were on the road ten minutes later. The day was just beginning and already I was feeling like a million.

Tomorrow I was sure to be closing deals that would add more money to the family coffers, but I now knew a feeling that beat that hands down.

Funnily enough, I've never really had much use for money, I like making it, but after you've got the basics, there isn't really much more you can do with it. Now with them, I can think of a million things I can do with my bank account.

I held her hand as we drove while we both took turns answering the boys' questions and there were a lot.

She was tense for the first twenty minutes or so until she relaxed and just enjoyed the view out the window.

When we came to the first place I actually grew nervous, what if she didn't like any of the ones I chose?

I kept up a running conversation, just pointing out the houses as we drove by, slowing down enough for her to get a good look.

It was the third one that caught her attention. I knew it by the way she craned her neck to get a better look and the way her pulse jumped in her wrist.

I pretended to be enjoying the architecture, while I asked her about the color of the stone and the grounds that consisted of a massive lawn with a garden that could barely be made out from the street.

I was pleased that she seemed reluctant to leave the area, but if I hung around there much longer I was afraid she'd figure me out and that might sour her on the idea.

I already knew exactly what I was going to do, how I was going to work it. It had taken me only one day to figure her out. Thank fuck she didn't have any hidden pockets; I've dealt with enough of that shit to last me a lifetime.

Chapter EIGHT

BRETT

The beach wasn't crowded as yet and I found a nice spot for us to spread the blanket that we'd brought. The boys were and handful from the time their little feet touched sand, and their only interest, was in the water.

Between the two of us they kept us hopping and I have to admit I was ass tired within an hour maybe. "How do you do it?" the little rascals were having a snack and chattering away at each other, which they do a lot of I noticed.

I'll have to keep an eye on that as they get older, who knows what the fuck they might be getting up to with that secret code shit they seem to be speaking.

Laurie says it's just baby talk, but I'm not too sure. I was a boy once, with brothers. Speaking of which, I need to call and rub it in that I beat them in the grandbaby race.

Since they're older they've beaten me at pretty much everything else, but this was a biggie.

"You have to prioritize. In the beginning, especially when they first started walking, it was rough. I jumped each time one of them moved. I was always afraid they would fall and hurt themselves.

I was constantly moving, never a dull moment. But then I got the hang of it and stopped being afraid, now I just watch and let them play with my heart in my throat. I guess it's always going to be that way as a mom. Do you have kids?"

She asked the last as if she thought she was overstepping. Hah, she can ask me anything, in fact I want her to.

"No, no kids, speaking of which, where's their dad?" The word damn near burnt a hole in my tongue.

"He's gone." She shifted sand through her fingers and gazed off over the water. "He's never even met them, but I don't blame him, not anymore. We were young, well I was two years younger, but he was still a kid himself."

"But do you think he'll come back one day, want to have a part in their lives?"

"I don't see how, he's never been here for them. I think I would be pissed if he showed up at some later date after all the ground work has been done you know."

"Yeah I hear you, so there's no way you'd go back to him?"

"Are you nuts? I wouldn't do that to my boys. As young as he was, I was younger; I stuck it out, he could've too. No, the boys don't need that kind of influence in their lives."

"What if he came back seeking custody at some later date?"

"I'll fight him to the death before I'd ever let that happen. No judge in their right mind would ever do that after what he's done."

You might be surprised. I didn't say that out loud, but the reality was that the justice system could be fucked sometimes and you never knew what was going to happen.

Especially if the judge was one of those asshole types that believed kids belonged with both parents, no matter how fucked they were.

"You said yesterday that you want to go back to school full time, what is it you want to study?"

"Right now I'm just taking the prerequisites for when I can go, that way they will be out of the way. I was actually thinking of early childhood development, I want to be a teacher. Either that or a daycare provider." She shrugged her shoulders and looked away again.

"And that's your dream?"

"No actually, my dream, before all this happened, was to grow up, meet prince charming, get married and have a ton of kids. I've never really been career oriented. But now with the boys, I have to face reality."

Damn this was sounding better and better. If she'd said it was her lifelong dream to be a career woman, I would've found a way to live with it.

But the reality is, I make more than enough money so that my wife wouldn't have to lift a finger to do anything, and quite frankly I don't want my woman working outside the home; something else to file away for future reference.

I fished for more information while we ran after the boys and played catch with them or built sand castles.

Before you know it, it was naptime and the boys were getting cranky. We packed up and headed back after feeding them the fruit and snacks she'd brought for their lunch.

I'd just spent three hours with them and it felt like nothing, like I could do it all day and not grow weary of it. My adrenaline was pumping like the time my brothers and I climbed Everest. I was definitely a goner.

We passed by the house again and although she was a little tired, she still smiled at it and watched out the window until it was out of sight.

I didn't miss the touch of sadness that left her when we turned the corner and it was no longer in view. She probably thought she'd never see it again.

Back at her place I helped her get the boys to bed. "I have something to do baby, how about I go take care of that and I'll be back with dinner later?"

"You don't have to do that..."
"I want to, what would the boys like? There's this really nice Italian place I know that have the best spaghetti and meatballs."

"Oh they'd love that thanks, are you sure?" I pulled her into me for a much needed kiss. She took me under as soon as our tongues met. Each time I took her mouth, it got harder and harder to let her go.

"You're so soft and sweet baby. What time is it?" she checked her watch and told me.

"Thirteen days, six hours to go, damn that seems so long all of a sudden. You said before that you only trust your dad to babysit..."

"Oh that's outside the babysitter I take them to. She doesn't work weekends so dad usually helps out then."

"So you only work during the week?"
"Yeah, which is a bummer because the restaurant gets busier on the weekend, but hey, you take what you can get right." Not for long, and not if I have anything to say about it.

I felt even surer of myself and what I was about to do when I left her. This had to be right, there's no way life could be so unfair as to put this woman in my way and not let me have her.

The realtor wasn't too put out about a last minute call on a Sunday. Especially not when I gave him my name.

After a quick clean up to get the sand off, and a little rough housing with my dog, I was back on the road and headed for her dream house.

The place looked even better up close, and the inside was a thing of beauty. There was more than enough room with five bedrooms and six bathrooms, and the backyard was plenty big enough for my rough and tumble boys to play in.

I could already see us here. I'll have to give the boys swimming lessons even though the large in-ground pool was gated.

Would she be happy here? She's the one that would be spending her days here while me and the boys went about school and work.

And I can't believe that I'm actually standing here contemplating this shit. Just a few short days ago I was ready to write off women.

Someone that I had grown to trust had betrayed me in the worst way and when she didn't get what she wanted, she'd gone to great lengths to destroy me.

A man in my position couldn't afford to have certain blemishes on his record and the one she tried to leave me with was a doozy.

It was the last straw in a long line of bullshit that I'd had to put up with lately and I was at the end of my rope.

So it's amazing that I find myself in the position of asking someone else to trust me with their future, their happiness.

But it felt right; I won't falter now, I'm gonna go with my gut all the way and see where it takes me.

"We'll take it." I'll leave the decorating and shit to her, but there was no reason I couldn't get started on some things.

By the time we were through with paperwork and all that we could get done on a Sunday, it was time for me to grab dinner. I called it in and picked it up on the way back to her.

Now how was I going to let her know what I'd done? I'm pretty sure she was going to be pissed if I just came right out and told her that I'd bought us a house, so I have to be slick.

I called her on the way back to her place to let her know I was almost there. I felt more excitement than I had in a long time, which only made me doubly sure that I was on the right track, not much gets a rise out of me these days.

The thoughts that had been plaguing me this last week threatened to intrude again, but I knocked them back, they had no place here.

I pulled up to her place and ran up the stairs, dying to see them again like I hadn't just left them a few short hours ago.

"Do you ever do anything small?" This was her question when she saw the bags of food I'd brought.

Since it wasn't dinnertime quite yet I decided to hang with the boys, who were still a little tired from the beach even after their naps.

It hurt my heart a little the way they fought for my attention, the way they sucked it up, because I knew what it meant. They were starved for male companionship. Her father was probably the only one they were ever around.

It hurt because for some fucked up reason I imagined what their lives would be like without me, if someone else came along, someone less trustworthy who was only out to use, to hurt.

The thought made my guts hurt, but it made me even more determined.

We played with building blocks and whatever else they could think of while one or the other took turns sitting on my lap and regaling me with tale after tale.

"Okay you three, time for dinner."

"Alright boys let's go wash up." I herded them into the bathroom that was barely big enough to hold me. I sneered and gritted my teeth, but held my tongue.

I can't forget how she'd stood up to me yesterday with her cute self, and had no doubt she'd tear me a new one if I criticized her home.

My disdain wasn't for her, I am proud of her for all that she's achieved so far on her own. I just wanted to give her, them, so much more and soon.

Almost as soon as we sat down to eat, the doorbell rang and she got up to answer it. Some guy came in, hugged her and kissed the top of her head, and to make matters worse, the boys were fighting to get down from their chairs to go to him.

As you can imagine I was more than a little pissed the fuck off, and to add insult to injury, the fucker saw my reaction and fucking smirked at me.

I have to admit it was not my finest moment. I was at the point of calling her out, seriously, me. Mr. calm, cool and collected, was ready to strangle her ass in front of the stranger and the boys.

I didn't even look at her, just kept my eyes on him as I left my seat and walked to where she was standing in front of him.

I didn't miss the fucker's grin when I put my arm around her and pulled her back into me, or the way she looked up at me like I'd lost my damn mind.

“Dad, this is Brett, Brett, my father Alan Payne.” Shit, no wonder he was laughing at me, he probably did that shit on purpose.

“Sir, pleased to meet you.” We shook hands and he walked over to say hello to his grandsons.

“Why don’t you join us for dinner dad? Brett brought enough food to feed an army.”

“If you’re sure you don’t mind.” He addressed this question to me and I was quick to assure him that it was fine by me. I got the impression the night before that he might not be too averse to his daughter dating someone, and who better than me? Maybe I could enlist his help if she proved to be too ornery.

“So Cantone, what brought you to my daughter’s neck of the woods? I don’t believe this is your playing field is it.”

"No, but the park where we met is between here and my place so..." He sat down across from me and fixed a plate.

The boys were talking his ear off, in fact they were telling him about Gunther and me from what little I could piece together.

He was studying me discretely, which was fine by me; he wouldn't be any kind of a cop if he didn't and an even worst father.

"So what's the verdict?" I asked him as soon as Laurie left the room to make coffee.

"I have one question then I'll let you know. What are your intentions?"

"I want to marry her."

"What about the boys?"

"They're mine." He gave me a very searching look, like I imagine he would a suspect in the interrogation room, but I didn't care, this shit was important, he could strip search me if it would get me closer to my goal.

"I think you should know, I already bought a house, she doesn't know yet though so don't mention it."

"Damn son, that's kinda fast isn't it? Though I can't say I'm surprised. I ran you of course, found out quite a lot. Everyone seems to like you, except those who oppose you in business. They say you're fair and just in your dealings until it comes to your enemies, then you're vicious.

I think you should know that if you do anything to harm my daughter or my grandkids I'll bury you. Money or not!"

"Fair enough, so does that mean that I have your blessing?"

"Not that I think you need it, but sure. Might I suggest you keep moving fast, if you give her time to think she'll make you both crazy, just overwhelm her if you will, trust me it's the only way."

"I kinda figured that."

"So I see."

She came back into the room then so we had to table our little discussion so I made a note to myself to contact him at a more opportune time.

She gave us a look of suspicion but didn't say anything as she retook her seat. We kept the conversation light after that and she was none the wiser.

Alan hung around playing with the boys for a while and I helped her clean up in the kitchen. I could hear the three of them laughing and whispering in the other room, and even that felt right.

"Did you think about what we talked about?" I passed her the dish to dry and kept the fact that there was barely enough room for both of us to myself.

I was walking a very tightrope here. On the one hand, I wanted to point out all that was missing in her life, to make myself look like a better prospect. And on the other, I didn't want her to think that she wasn't doing a good job.

If I took our relationship out and looked at it realistically, I knew it didn't make sense. No woman in her right mind, especially one with two little hearts to protect, would ever just jump right in.

But I didn't want to wait, couldn't stand the thought of waiting. "What would you say if I told you I wanted you and the boys to come home with me?"

She stopped wiping the dish and stared at me. "I know you have to be practical, I know this all seems crazy, but think about it from my point of view.

I met this amazing woman with two beautiful little tykes who stole my heart in one day. I have more than enough of everything to make their lives easier, but she won't let me because she's afraid.

So I have to leave her tonight and every night, because I plan on seeing them every single day, and go back to my lonely condo, leaving them here unprotected."

"You do know we've lived on our own for tow years without incident."
"That's not the point and you know it."

"You said it yourself, it's not very realistic for you to expect me to just jump into the situation no matter how much I may want to."

"So you do want to." I dropped the dish back in the soapy water and snatched her up. "Well what's stopping you?"

"Put me down before dad comes in here, he's nosy."

"Uh-uh, tell me, what's stopping you? Is it fear of the unknown? I could say the same you know. I'm worth billions, how do I know you won't take me for all I've got?"

"How would I do that?"

"When I marry you, you will be entitled to half my assets, and when you get to know me you'll learn that I hate to lose, so you see, we both have something to lose."

"Somehow I don't think it's the same. I don't think you can compare paper to a broken heart."

"Who says you won't break my heart? You stand as much chance of breaking my heart as I do yours. Or are you one of those women who think that men have no feelings and are only interested in one thing?"

She bit her lip and seemed to be giving my words some thought. "You know what your problem is baby, you think too much. Let's take a chance on each other."

"If it were just me, but the boys..."

"Don't you see? This is as much for them, as it is for us. I just met them yesterday and I'm already in love with them. I want to give them everything that I had as a kid..."

"That's just it, how can I trust that? How can I believe that you want my boys when their own father has never even seen them?"

"I thought I told you I wasn't about to pay for some other asshole's fuck ups? He was a kid you said right? I don't know why he ran, but I'll tell you what, I'm happy as fuck that he's out of the picture.

I don't know what I would've done if you'd told me that you were taken. I've never reacted this way to anyone before in my life. Not mentally or physically.

The bottom line here is that I will always be a part of your life from now on. I will never let anyone else have you ever, so you're pretty much stuck.

Now I'm trying to respect you and give you the time you need, but it's going to be hard. If you drag this shit out it's going to be torture."

"We've known each other a little more than twenty four hours, you're acting as if I've been stringing you along for months or something."

"It feels like fucking forever already and knowing your stubborn ass it'll take you that long to get your shit together. Here's what we're going to do.

I'll give you time to get to know me, but no space."

"What does that mean?" she frowned up at me before wiping the forgotten dish in her hand.

"It means that I'm going to be here with you every minute that you're not at work. I want to spend as much time as possible with you and the boys until you're all comfortable with me.

I'll try not to rush you into bed, but I will touch you at every opportunity. With that said, the two weeks rule still stands so I hope you get whatever it is you need before then, because Laurie I promise you, that is the one thing I will not give in on."

"What if I say no?"
"You won't"
"How can you be so sure?"
"Because by then I would have won you over, I already have the boys so that's done. Just think about it okay."

Chapter NINE

It felt like something was off when I went to the office the next day. Like I was missing a limb. I wasn't at my desk five minutes before I was reaching for the phone.

I'd already spoken to the boys this morning when I woke up, and I know she starts work in another hour, but I missed her like hell already.

I changed course and did something I've never done for anyone else but mom. "Hey Mel, this is Brett Cantone, I need a couple dozen pink roses delivered."

"Pink, but your mom likes yellow roses." Oh shit, I guess I know who her next call will be. Why didn't I think of that? Oh well, too late now.

"These aren't for mom, and Mel, I need them to go out ASAP." I gave her the name and address and hung up.

Five minutes later mom was crowing on the phone. "Pink huh, so she's a girly girl?"

"Mom, I'm working here."
"You're not too busy to order roses you can spare me a minute or two. So, anything new there, have you made any progress?"

"Mom we just met two days ago what do you expect?"
"With you, I thought for sure we'd be heading to the delivery room at least."

"Very funny mom, but I've promised to give Laurie time to get use to the idea of us."

"How many days did you give her?" Damn, she really does know her kids like she's been saying all these years.

"I was feeling magnanimous, I gave her two weeks." She made me grin with her antics.

"Atta boy, so what's the game plan?" I shared a few of the details with her, kind of like a sounding board I guess; but it was only after I hung up the phone that I realized she'd pumped me for information. Sneak.

The phone rang twenty minutes later and I grinned like an ass when I saw that it was Laurie. "Hello sweetheart."

"Hi again, they're beautiful thanks, but you've done so much already..."

"Ah-ah-ah, you're not doing that anymore remember. I'm showing you the kind of life I want to offer you. I understand your fear sweetie, trust me, I do, but I want you to believe that I'm not going to change once I get you into my bed.

Now how about we take the boys out to eat tonight?" Can't stay on one topic for too long with this one, or she'd beat it to death.

"Uh, I'm not sure that's such a good idea, we don't do too much of that, they're not that good at sitting still for long as you well know."

"Fine, then have dinner with me at my place, the three of you. It's either that or a restaurant, lady's choice."

"That's not really much of a choice now is it? I have to go Brett I don't wanna be late, and thanks again for the flowers."

"Good then it's settled, my place, I'll pick you up at four, that's when you get the boys right?"

"Yes but..."
"No buts babe, call your dad and tell him where you'll be. I'm sure he has my address but just in case pass it on." I gave her my address before hanging up, not giving her any more time to come up with another excuse.

The day couldn't go by fast enough for me and by the time three o'clock rolled around I was heading for the door.

I couldn't remember one fucking thing I'd done all day. I think I stopped trying to get anything done when I caught myself doodling like a fucking eight-year old girl.

"You can knock off early Casey, as soon as you've finished working on the Scarponi deal."

"Okay sir, uh, is there an emergency?" She looked at me like she was seeing a stranger for the first time.

"Nope." I knew why she was asking. In all the years she's worked for me, I've never left the office before her.

I planned to change that in the near future as well. Since the boys were still young, and I was plotting and scheming to get their mother with child as soon as possible, she was going to need all the help she could get.

Daddy was going to have to take a very hands-on approach, so might as well start from now. I can do pretty much everything from home these days anyway, so no loss there.

I rushed home first and got out of my work clothes. Since it was a spur of the moment thing I had to check the cupboards to see what I had that was appropriate for their little palates.

I was stumped so I called the one person I knew would be of help to me.

"Mom, what do you feed three year old boys?" She got a good laugh out of that one and then tried to weasel an invite out of me, which I ignored.

"Okay, since you don't want your old mom to help you out. You can't go wrong with mac and cheese."

"No good, they had pasta yesterday from Luigi's. I just remembered, they haven't eaten a vegetable in two days so maybe something healthy?"

"Certainly you can add some vegetables to the meal, but they're not going to eat just that. Do you have any chicken in the freezer?"

I opened the door and looked. She knew damn well that I did since she put it there. For some reason she doesn't trust me to take care of myself, so once a month, whether I've done the grocery shopping or not, she does one of her own.

"I have boneless breasts in here." "Very good, now you're going to want to bread those and fry them like chicken fingers, kids love that stuff and you can always do something different with yours and Laurie's. You sure you don't want me to run over and help you out?"

"No thanks mom you'll meet them soon enough I promise, love you bye, gotta run."

I put the chicken to defrost and dug through the vegetable bin for some broccoli. I know kids hate this stuff, but my boys are gonna learn to eat healthy from a young age, just the way I was raised.

My boys, I love the sound of that. With most of the prep ready I checked my watch and dried my hands. It was time to go get my little family. I gave the house a quick glance over to make sure everything was neat.

"Gunther, we're having company, I want you to be on your best behavior okay." He barked once for yes and that was good enough for me.

It seemed stupid to be this excited about taking them home for dinner, but it felt like the best thing I'd done in a long time.

I rang the doorbell and waited as I heard the boys calling for me from behind the door. I guess she'd told them I was coming.

They rushed me as soon as the door was open and I picked them both up and hugged them close. I felt them in my heart, like this was supposed to be.

"I missed you guys." I inhaled the scent from their little heads as she looked on indulgently, good; at least that look of wariness wasn't as prevalent as it had been. Progress.

"You ready baby?" She nodded and grabbed her mommy's bag that seemed to hold everything, and we were out the door with a boy in each of my arms.

" So, boys, how was your day?" They chattered away at me, some I understood some not so much. Their mother and I shared a smile and I reached for her hand and raised it to my lips for a kiss.

Gunther was kicking up a fuss before I even got the door open when we reached, and it was sheer pandemonium once the boys were inside.

The three of them hit the rug while Laurie stood in the doorway looking around. "What's the matter?"

"Your house, it's so nice, do you have any idea what my boys can do in a place like this in ten minutes flat?"

I looked around at my place, trying to see what she saw, but I couldn't. Sure I had nicer things, so what, it's not like it was the Smithsonian.

"Relax Laurie, if you relax they'll relax, let's go into the kitchen. Would you like some wine?"

"Uh, I've never really had any, still underage remember?" that was so strange; she's old enough to have a child, but not to have wine.

"We probably shouldn't with the boys anyway so scratch that. I have some cookies and milk for their after school snack unless you've already given them something."

"No, you got there three minutes after we did so I haven't had time.

"Good, I'll get them." I was trying to find things to occupy myself so that I didn't jump her.

For the past two days I've only seen her in jeans or sweats. Both showed off her amazing ass, but today she'd changed up on me.

Today she wore a dress. It was short and flirty, one of those summer things that blow in the wind and left her shoulders bare.

She looked young and fresh and so fucking fuckable it was hard not to pounce. I took the boys their snack and muzzled Gunther just to be safe.

I was pretty sure he wouldn't hurt the boys, but I wasn't taking any chances, I can't forget what he really is after all.

While they were preoccupied, I went back to the kitchen and grabbed her hand, pulling her into the laundry room and closing the door halfway. I didn't want little eyes seeing what I was about to do.

I took her mouth before she could question me; her taste went straight to my head. I let my hands roam free along her legs, up to her thighs and back down.

Her nipples were already little points, poking into my chest as we dueled with our tongues.

"Fuck I missed you, what're you doing to me?" I only left her lips long enough to breathe out those words before I went back for more.

This time I let my hands roam farther up beneath her dress until I reached the heat between her thighs. The soft silk of her underwear was no barrier against my marauding fingers; I had to feel her.

I slipped my fingers into her slowly, one after the other. My heart beat out of control in my chest as I worked my fingers in and out of her.

She did what she always does when I touch her, only this time I got to feel the liquid heat as it gushed out of her into my palm.

She moved against my hand as her pussy quivered around the fingers that I used to fuck her through her next orgasm.

"Brett." Fuck, her voice had that sexy 'just fucked' quality to it.
"Shh, they'll hear you." I left my hand between her legs and lifted her dress all the way up with the other. "Move your bra, I wanna taste you."

She very shyly and ever so slowly lowered her bra cup and let her nipple spring free and right into my waiting mouth.

I double-teamed her then, driving my fingers into the softness of her pussy, as I sucked hard on her tit. When she started moving against my hand faster, I added more pressure, letting my palm press into her clit as I finger fucked her harder.

When she squeezed down and started to cum again I knew I had to taste her, her scent was driving me mad.

Pulling my fingers out of her, I released her nipple and dropped to the floor between her feet. Thank fuck she wasn't wearing too much.

All I had to do was pull her underwear down and off, before clamping my mouth over her sweet spot. Her juices flooded my mouth as her fingers clutched at my hair.

I sucked and nibbled at her flesh until she couldn't take anymore. I think she was dry by the time I wiped my mouth off on her thigh and stood. "You've got a problem."

I had nothing left she had taken it all. There was no fucking way, no way.

"Wha, what's that?" it was good to see that she was flustered as well, but I was about to make her life even more difficult than I already had.

Just what the fuck had I been playing at? I've gone harder for less. Things that at the end of the day didn't add up to a hill of beans, I've fought tooth and nail for.

And now this, what could be the most important thing in my life; I was leaving up to someone else, fuck that.

It's time this little mother met the real me. She was going to be spending the rest of her life with him anyway so might as well.

"I have to break a promise that I made to you. I said I would give you time, I can't. You're not going home."

"What, are you insane?"

"Maybe, but I'm pretty sure I'm not. Let's get dinner ready then afterwards I have something to show you and the boys.

Feel free to call your dad if you start to panic, but it's a done deal. Your taste, I've never tasted anything like you and I'm pretty sure there's a reason for that. I'm not waiting Laurie, fuck that."

I didn't hang around for the argument, just left her to fix herself while I went and saw about dinner for my little family.

She wasn't doing much better by the time she joined me a little while later. "Can I help?" I checked her over to make sure she was really okay.

Other than looking a little flushed, it didn't look like I'd given her heart failure.

"No, you've been on your feet all day, sit."
"Brett, you know we can't do this right?" Here it comes.

"I know no such thing. What I do know is that I'm a man, you're a woman and we want each other. Uh-uh-uh let me finish. If it were just a matter of sex, it wouldn't be this hard on both of us, but it's because we both want more.

You think you're the only one with something to lose, you're wrong. In only a matter of three days, I can tell you I have no idea what I would do if I lost you and the boys, I can't see it.

In three days I've felt things in my heart and even done things that I would never have imagined.

There's something that you don't know about me, I don't give up when there's something that I want, and baby, I have never in my life wanted anything as much as I want you.

And Laurie, the end all and be all is this, I will not let you fuck up our lives because you're too scared to take a chance, now go get our boys."

She slinked out of the kitchen and I figured I was onto something. She didn't seem to have much argument left; either that or she was plotting her escape from the crazy man. Whatever, she wasn't going anywhere.

It didn't matter one wit to me what others would think or how soon it was. I know what I know, fuck everything else.

There were no real obstacles standing in our way, well except for fear, and that wasn't going to stop me. I'll just have to prove to her that life can be a fairytale sometimes.

I cut the boys' food up so that it would cool faster and turned my attention to our own dinner, while she oversaw them at the table.

Gunther stood guard and ate whatever scraps they fed him, which consisted mostly of the green stuff.

Dinner was noisy and fun as was to be expected, but it wasn't over long before I was ushering them out the door.

"Come on little mama, I want to show you something remember?" We got the boys cleaned up and downstairs.

I kept her distracted with small talk as we drove, but she had her eyes peeled out the window as the boys carried on their usual jibber jabber in the backseat.

"Where are we going, it's a bit late for the beach isn't it?" We were halfway to our destination. She hadn't brought up our conversation but I didn't fool myself that she'd given in that easily.

"We're not going to the beach love just hang on we're almost there." She looked back out the window as I drove.

"Here we are." Her eyes widened on me when I pulled in through the gate. With the sun setting behind it, lighting up the stone, it was even more beautiful than yesterday.

"Brett?" She called out to me as I reached for the door handle and I looked back at her.
"It's ours."
"It's..."

I got out of the jeep before she could say anything more and walked around to the back.

I released my dog first, who seemed to know what all that extra yard space was for, and then went after the boys in their car seats.

By now she was out and on the other side getting Dmitri while I got Garrett. I tossed her the keys when we were both finished getting the boys.

"You do the honors." She was still a little flummoxed but her reflexes were good and she caught them.

"This is insane, we can't do this." She was panicking again but I was prepared for that. Once I'd made up my mind to take over and not leave my fate up to her, it was easier to deal with the situation.

"Look at our boys." They were already rolling around in the grass with the dog, fucking picture perfect. I knew she would argue me to death but I had something for her little ass.

I'll let her talk all she wanted to, but there was no way I was easing up on her. Shit, if I was willing to take a chance then so should she, no more of this nice guy bullshit, it wasn't gonna get me what I want.

Like I said, I'd let her talk things out of course, but the end result was going to be the same either way. After tonight, we won't ever be apart again.

"Let's go inside, come on boys and bring the dog with you." I was pretty sure the dog was no longer mine. At least he was trained to protect so I wouldn't have to worry about my boys when I was away.

Her hands shook when she opened the door, but I picked her up and took her over the threshold.

The place was empty, just bare walls and shining marble floors. The ceilings were high and there were enough wrap around windows to let in the natural light.

"There are more than enough bedrooms and bathrooms, and a nursery, more than enough room for the family we're going to have."

"Just how many children are you planning to have?" Huh, if I tell you it'll scare the shit out of you, no way.

"We'll discuss that at a later date. Let's walk through and see what you like and don't like. We can hire a decorator, or you can do it all yourself, that's up to you."

"Oh I'd love to do it my..." She caught herself and cut herself off, but it was too late.

"So that's what we'll do then." I put my arm around her shoulders and led her from room to room as the boys and the dog scampered around slipping and sliding on the floors.

"We should stop at one of those kiosks and get some magazines, unless you prefer to look on line. Whatever you choose is fine by me, just don't wait too long to get started."

"Are you always this rash? What if this doesn't work out? Then you would've spent all that money for nothing."

Time to bring out the big guns. "Do me a favor, close your eyes, they closed, good. Imagine me here with a woman and children, now imagine that that woman isn't you."

I saw her flinch just like she'd done in the park when I told her we could go our separate ways.

"Good, I see you don't like that idea. The house is bought, no matter what it's going to be my home. You can either share it with me, or leave the door open for someone else to walk through, your call."

I gave her some time to let that shit sink in before putting her out of her misery.

"Just remember, I'm not letting you go, so I'm not sure how you're supposed to pull that one off."

Her sigh of relief did not go unnoticed and gave me hope. I pulled her into me for a kiss while the boys ran and screamed around the house, with the dog at their heels.

We were there for hours, because as unsure as she was of my sincerity, she loved that house.

We finally had to leave because it was getting late and we both had work the next day, not to mention the boys were starting to lag.

I almost didn't want to take her home to get clothes for her and the boys, because I was afraid that she would balk at my command that she come home with me once we got there.

As we pulled up to her place I switched off the ignition and turned to her. She looked like she was ready to bolt at the slightest provocation.

"Listen, you can sleep in the guestroom if you'd like so long as we share the same roof.

I want you under me as soon as fucking possible, but I want all of you more. So I'll wait the two weeks that I gave you, if you choose to make me suffer."

That seemed to work because she visibly relaxed before looking back at the boys. "I'll be right back."

"Wait." I got out and went around to help her. "It'll be fine baby, I promise you that." I kissed her forehead and gave her a little squeeze before watching her walk away.

She was gone long enough just to gather up some stuff, while I sat downstairs in the jeep with the boys and tried to get a grip. Not even my first solo deal had made me sweat as much.

I didn't breathe easy until I saw her coming back and I got out to help her.

The ride back was a little tense, but I kept up a running conversation with her and the boys who were on their last legs.

Back in the condo I helped set up the boys' room which had only one bed, but they were too tired to fight.

They begged to watch one of their kiddie movies before bedtime, which I loaded up for them. "Call your dad."

"Why?" She took the phone that I passed to her.

"Because I want you to be comfortable here. I know this is fast and I wish I could get you to understand why I want this, but you have to admit that somewhere deep inside, you know that this is going to be good, or else you wouldn't be here right now.

I know you would never put the boys in danger, even if you don't. You're afraid of being a bad mom, of making a mistake that might cost them; still here you are, and do you know why?

Because you know, in here," I put my hand over the place where her heart beat, "that this was meant, and you want this for them too."

She put the phone down without dialing and I pulled her in for a kiss. "Thank you."

Chapter TEN

It's been three days Brett; give her time. I kept repeating those words in my head over and over again as I paced the floor of my bedroom.

We'd put the boys to bed a short while ago and she'd shyly gone into the room I'd shown her to, leaving me out in the cold.

I wish I were the type to celebrate the huge victory of actually having her safe under my roof, of being able to walk down the hall and look in on the boys. I can close my eyes tonight and not worry about something happening to them while they sleep away from me.

But no; I want it all, as incongruous as that is, I don't think I will be happy until I have it all exactly as I want it.

She's turned me into one of those assholes that walk around with their tongue hanging out, at least that's how I was beginning to feel.

I don't get it. I've waited longer for a woman to make up her mind. in fact, I've never rushed any woman into my bed, seeing as how I myself have never been into one night stands.

With Laurie, I felt like if I didn't get into her soon, something was going to come along and snatch her away from me.

And beyond all that, I want to get so deep inside her, it hurts just to think about it.

"Fuck this." I marched from my room down the hall to her door, and without knocking, walked right in. I came up short at the sight of her asleep on the bed.

"So fucking beautiful." I hadn't meant to say the words out loud, but thankfully, they were low enough that I did not disturb her, not before I did what I came here for anyway.

I removed the sheet that she had covering her and felt my cock jump at my first look at her almost naked. She was barely wearing some short lacy thing that was too long for underwear and too short for shorts, with a silky looking top to match.

She was so fucking tiny when I picked her up; she hardly weighed anything. "What?" She started to come awake.

"Shh, go back to sleep, another change of plans." She came fully awake when I put her in my bed and came down beside her. "Stay." I rested my hand on her hip to keep her in my bed.

"I'll try not to touch you, but I can't fucking sleep in here with you in there." I pulled her over to me and wrapped my arms around her, with her half on my chest.

"There, maybe now I can get some sleep." She was stiff as a board for a good five minutes before she realized that I wasn't about to take her against her will.

"Are you settled now? Because I'm about to kiss you and I don't want you to freak." I lifted her chin so that I could get to her mouth.

What we shared was more a devouring than anything as innocent as a kiss. She just went the fuck up in flames as soon as my tongue touched hers.

I pulled her fully on top of me and let her legs spread out over mine, putting her pussy right over the ridge of my cock.

While my mouth took control of hers, I moved her up and down my rod with my hands on her hips as guides. She might have doubts about happily ever after, but her body sure knew what it wanted.

“Please let me have you; fuck do you feel that?” I think my cock was harder and longer than it’s ever been before.

I turned us over until I was dry humping her and my cock was leaking all over us. "I need to get inside you, right fucking now." You promised Brett, fuck that.

"Brett, I'm scared." Still she followed my mouth with hers as she tried to keep contact between my dick and her pussy.

"Don't be, I won't hurt you I promise; please trust me." I was removing her sexy shorts as I spoke, making sure to touch her in all the right places to keep her primed.

I could barely hold onto my cock as I wrestled it out of my pajama bottoms. I should stop and take care of her, get her body ready for me, but I wasn't about to give her a chance to call a halt.

Instead I touched her wet core with the tip of my cock, rubbed it up and down her slit a few times, and then found her mouth with my own again.

"Mine!" I growled the word into her mouth as I pushed into her, going slowly at first because I knew how inexperienced she was.

Hot, wet silk surrounded my iron hard cock and made him feel ever so welcome. She had a little trouble taking all of me, so I took my time and worked all eleven inches into her, until there was none left to feed her.

"Fuck me." Lifting my chest from hers, I looked down at her in wonder. "Merciful fuck baby." I moved inside her, because I couldn't not move.

Whatever it was about her that drew me from the beginning, was nothing compared to what she made me feel as I was buried deep inside her sweet, cunt.

"I fucking knew it, look at me." She writhed beneath me in heat, her face a picture of sheer carnal pleasure.

"Look at me I said." I pounded into her and held. Her eyes finally opened as I pulled her head back. "This is mine, I don't care about anything else, hang-ups, fears, doubts. I don't give a fuck." Her eyes widened in surprise at my words; too bad.

"I will never let you keep yourself from me again, never, now kiss me." I didn't wait for her compliance, but took her mouth hungrily.

I think I lost it there for a few seconds. My mind was full of visions of me humbling her beneath me. All the different ways I was going to mount her in the future played through my head.

I nipped her lip first, before leaving her mouth and kissing and licking my way down her neck until I caught her flesh between my teeth to mark her in the most obvious way.

Her body fit perfectly beneath me, as she moved with me stroke for stroke, thrust for thrust. "Shit, are you protected?"

I had her bent almost double with her legs up to her ears as I fucked her with hard, deep strokes.

"Uh-huh, I'm on the pill." For the first time in my life, those words were disappointing, but they didn't stop me from fucking into her. I'll deal with that later.

Right now I was too busy trying to catalogue my every emotion. I wanted to remember every feel every sound, everything breath. Nothing had ever felt this good. It was as if she were made to fit around me.

Pretty soon nice and easy wasn't enough anymore and I found myself lifting her sweet little ass in my hands and pulling her onto my cock rougher.

There was something deep inside her that teased the tip of my cock each time I went into her. The next time I went deep I knocked against it and pushed through.

She screamed around my tongue as the tight ring snapped around my dick and held me captive.

Her cervix, good now I know where I will be going every time I take her. “Did I hurt you?” I brushed the hair back from her face as I held still until she got comfortable.

“No, I just feel so full.” I kissed her until she relaxed again under me, then I started moving in her.

I don’t think she ever stopped cumming from the moment I entered her. “Are you ready?” I eased up and out before turning her onto her knees and pulling her ass high.

I studied the pink of her pussy because I wanted to remember everything about that too, before sliding home.

If I thought she felt good before, the feel of her from behind was out of this fucking world. “Move on my cock baby.”

I reveled in her innocence when she first started moving against me. She really had only done this once.

That thought led to another and it was as if someone turned a switch in my head. The most fucked up feeling ran through me then and I pulled out of her, afraid that I might do something stupid. What the fuck was that?

My cock was screaming to cum, he was so close. But there was something fucked up going on in my head and my heart.

It scared me with its intensity and its newness. I've never felt it before, but I knew it was a danger to her.

"What's the matter?" Her eyes were wide and full of worry, as if she thought she'd displeased me. You are so fucked Brett.

"I need to know about their fa...about the guy you...fuck."

I got off the bed and paced around the room with fistfuls of my hair in my hands. "I need to know about the boy you were with."

"What about him?" She looked confused and a little apprehensive as she tried to get the sheets to cover herself, and no wonder. If half of what I was feeling was showing on my face, she must be scared out of her fucking mind.

"Did you love him?" What the fuck are you doing Brett? I hadn't seen any of this coming, but it was here and I had to deal with it.
"I, we were kids Brett."

"That's not what I asked you, did you think you were in love with him?"

"I guess so in the beginning but..." I gave her a nasty look, that's how fucked my head was in that moment.

"Why did he leave?"
"Brett you're scaring me, what's this all about?" I just looked at her until she realized I wasn't going to say anything else until she answered me.

"He left because he was afraid he'd get into trouble for getting me pregnant I guess."

"So if he hadn't ran you'd still be with him?"
"I don't know, how can I answer that?" And that was the fucking problem, she had no answers and I needed one.

Walking back over to the bed I stood looking down at her before getting on top of her.

I knocked her legs open with my knee and shoved into her. Grabbing a fistful of her hair, I pulled her head back.

"I fucking hate that he had you, I hate that anyone else has ever touched you. I'm sorry if this hurts you but I want to erase him from your fucking memory."

I have no idea what the fuck was wrong with me, where the raw emotion was coming from. All I know is that I wanted to consume her, to take her into me and bury myself deep into her until we became one.

She tried soothing me by running her hands up and down my back, but nothing was going to soothe whatever the fuck was wrong with me, until I bred her too.

I came hard as fuck on that thought and kept fucking until she creamed me again. Pulling out I dragged her into my side and wrapped myself around her.

"You okay?" I was still trying to catch my breath.

"Yeah, except for the part where you went crazy, we need to talk about that, if it's going to be a problem..."

"It's my thing, I'll deal with it." Thank fuck it didn't return any of the other times I pulled her under me that night and into the morning.

Chapter ELEVEN

"Wait, wait, wait, shh, don't move yet." The alarm had just gone off and she'd started to slip out of my arms, but I wasn't ready to let her go just yet. I hit the off button, now fully awake and took a moment to enjoy just the reality of having her here with me.

I turned her onto her back gently, and pulled her night shorts back down her legs. I didn't even have to guide my dick he sniffed her hole out himself and without any preamble slid right on in.

"Good morning." I went after the other side of her neck with my teeth as I rode her. She opened her legs and accepted me, and those same feelings from the night before slammed into me.

I concentrated on the feel of her silk walls around the heat of my cock. On the way her nails dug into my flesh as she moaned into my ear.

The way her pussy clenched around me when I sucked her flesh into my mouth to mark her, like she liked that shit.

"Stay home today, call in sick. We'll take the boys to daycare and come back here and stay in bed all day."

It's a minor miracle that I can talk while I'm inside her, all my other faculties seem to have left me.

"I don't know, I've never called in sick before unless it was for one of the boys." That wasn't an outright no, which in Laurie lingo means I can persuade her.

"Stay with me." She didn't have to know that in the next few days I was going to do my best to convince her that she should give up the job altogether.

I was sure that wasn't gonna go over too well, and I didn't want to spoil the nice glow we had going.

I used my dick to convince her. A few strokes in the right places, a finger on her clit and two teasing a nipple while I licked and bit her neck seemed to do the trick.

"Fine, I'll call in."
"Good." My real reason for wanting her to stay was twofold. It occurred to me that though I'd fucked my girl all night, I hadn't really made love to her. For the bond to be complete the way I needed it to be, I had to take her in every way possible.

And I don't think I could make it away from her this soon, I was pretty sure if I tried I wouldn't get shit done. I've become obsessed.

In the early morning hours as she'd drifted into sleep, I laid awake planning, and thinking.

My reaction to her was nowhere near anything I've ever known, and way more than expected. I knew without a doubt as I watched her chest rise and fall with each breath, that I was all the way fucking gone over this girl.

"I love you." I looked down at her as my cock throbbed inside her and she looked at me, still with doubt in her eyes. "I love you." I repeated the words because it felt good as fuck to say them. I'd lost my fucking mind on that park bench.

I covered her mouth and rocked into her slow and deep as her heart beat like a drum beneath mine as I emptied my nuts inside her for like the tenth time.

***

LAURIE

My life has gone off the rails somewhere. This isn't my life; it can't be can it? Why should this happen to me? Something that I'm sure happens very rarely just doesn't happen to people like me.

I watched him out the corner of my eye as he got out to help me out of the jeep. The boys were going crazy in the backseat and why not?

Brett had gone into their room just as they were about to get up and had spent a good part of the morning playing with them and the dog.

I was only just a little hurt when they chose him to help them get ready this morning instead of me. I guess if we were going to do this then I'd have to get use to sharing them.

It was amazing to watch them together, the way my boys just followed his lead, even the way they looked up at him as he spoke to them, like he'd hung the moon.

I still had that fear in my heart that something was gonna go wrong, it wasn't as strong as just a few short days ago, but it was there all the same.

It just didn't seem real that's all. And my boys were already sucked into him. They didn't even bat a lash when he told them they couldn't watch a cartoon while they ate the breakfast he'd made.

He acted as though this was nothing, having us move in here after only three days of knowing each other.

And what does that say about me? Oh shit what did I do? What kind of person am I..."

“What are you doing baby?” His voice pulled me back from the brink but that new fear was now beating in my chest like bird’s wings.

“Nothing, just thinking about things.”

“Yeah well whatever you’re thinking cut that shit out. I can read your face and I don’t like what I see, if you tell me you need others to validate who and what I am I’m going to be so pissed.

Come on boys let’s get cleaned up.” He helped them down from their chairs and let them run loose.

I was as nervous as a new mother, watching their every move, afraid that they would break something. Brett on the other hand seemed completely relaxed.

I wish I could be as relaxed as he was, but our realities were completely different. He wasn't the single mother of two who was barely making it, and stood to lose a hell of a lot if this thing went wrong.

But maybe I wasn't being fair to him either. Perhaps it was like he said and he had a lot to lose as well, I just didn't see it.

He's young, handsome and loaded, what could he possibly have to lose? I tried to keep all these thoughts hidden from him since he seemed to be able to read my mind along with everything else.

He still seemed to know what I was thinking and I soon found myself trapped between him and the wall, while he sent the boys and the dog on some kind of scavenger hunt.

"I want to care about what the fuck is going on in your head, I really do, but if it's going to fuck up what we have going on here, then you're fucked.

Just do me a favor, whenever those doubts rear their head, just tell yourself you don't have a choice, because you don't. You let me have you babe and it was so fucking good I'd go out on a limb and say a man would kill for less.

There are some things in life that once you find them, you hold on with everything you've got, and let nothing and no one come between.

You are that one thing for me; good luck with fucking with that. Now let's go, our boys are ready."

When he says things like that, with his face set in those lines, I want to jump him and run screaming at the same time.

Of course the ladies at the daycare were all aflutter at his presence, and I saw women's reaction to him for the first time. I didn't like it. Again he seemed oblivious, but it helped that he kept one of his hands on me at all times.

Even while he was answering their questions he had his hand on my ass and it seemed so natural, I didn't even think to object.

He raced back to the house after we were done, and I found myself hustled up the steps and my back up against the wall as soon as the door closed.

I always get a hitch in my breathing the first time he puts his hands on me and he looks at me like the words he says are for real.

I want so badly to reach out and take what he's offering, but something was holding me back. He picked me up and I wrapped my legs around him and pulled his mouth down to mine.

At least here I knew what to expect; pure pleasure if that was the word for it. I never knew one person could make another feel like this.

If he felt the things I felt when we touched then I could almost believe that he was for real.

***

BRETT

We made it to the bed by feeling along the walls because I wasn't about to release her mouth.

I fought out of my jeans and helped her get out of her clothes before tossing her playfully onto the bed.

"I'm going to eat you alive baby, hang on." I spread her out on the bed so I could look at her from head to toe. She was perfection, her skin silky soft under my rough hands as I ran them over her.

I spent some time getting acquainted with her nipples. They were sensitive to the touch of my hands and my tongue as I found out when I started to play.

"Hmm, you like breast play huh." She was almost purring just from my mouth suckling her.

Moving down her body, I lifted her knees up and back; making her face go up in flames, but I wanted her open for my tongue and fingers.

I placed teasing kisses along her thigh until I reached her sweet smelling pussy. One teasing lick from my tongue and I moved down the other leg, before starting all over again.

Her scent teased my nostrils my second time around and I opened her with my fingers. “Damn.” She had the prettiest fucking pussy in the world.

Reds and pinks, smooth. She was shaved bare leaving all of her exposed to my eyes.

My tongue actually stiffened in preparation for the taste of her. Again I closed my eyes to compute everything about the moment as I lowered my head to her.

If it’s true what they say, you are what you eat. Then she must eat every fucking sweet thing in the world.

Her taste, just like the feel and sight of her, was designed to drive me fucking nuts. I didn't just want to eat her pussy I wanted to attach the shit to my tongue.

If I were a fanciful being I would swear there was some kind of cosmic force at work here. There was no way she could be this fucking perfect.

Even the way she grabbed my hair and squeezed her legs around my head was different. I couldn't leave her pussy alone and in the back of my mind was the thought that it was a good thing I hadn't done this the night before or we wouldn't have made it out of bed this morning.

I actually growled into her pussy as I lifted her like an offering to my mouth, where I used my tongue to fuck her.

She came on my tongue while I played with her clit with my thumb. I had it all planned out in my head, I was going to eat her pussy for at least half an hour and then take my time and devour the rest of her.

I think I lasted five minutes before I was slamming into her. Her loud screech cleared the fog from my eyes and had me going stock-still.

She was cumming but I could tell I'd hurt her a little so I eased out of her cervix and comforted her with soft kisses along her cheek and forehead.

"Is it better now?" I moved a little when she tightened around me, letting me know that it was okay to move.

"Do you know what I think? I think you were meant for me. I think I was supposed to be in that park that day just to meet you and the boys.

You know what else I think? I think that whatever this is that's brought us here, would not let me be the only one feeling this.

I know you have to feel at least half of what I feel." I moved inside her as I held her head still so I could look at her as I spoke.

"And if you do then you need to let me know, because I'm about to speed this shit up again."

"What do you mean?" I love the way she tries to work my dick with her pussy when I stop moving inside her, like she can't fucking get enough; stills she's giving me shit.

"That thing last night, I don't know what it is, but I know that I won't be happy until I get you with child."

"You, what?" She stopped moving but I didn't.

"I know, crazy right, but like I said, if you feel half of what I'm feeling then you know this shit is real and you know what.

Everything is fucking perfect except I can't get the idea of this guy out of my head. I fucking hate that he was there before me.

That's a fucked up way to feel I know, and it in no way takes away from what the fuck I feel for you, but babe, it's killing me."

I'm not sure what men in my position usually did with this shit. I have no idea what my words are doing to her if anything.

I just know that for some reason, every time I get inside her, a switch goes off inside my head and all I can think of is erasing him from her life.

"You can't seriously be annoyed at something that happened before we even met."

"I think it has more to do with the fact that things weren't really resolved between you two." What the fuck kind of conversation is this to be having at a time like this?

"Brett, I don't know what you want from me here." Now we were both stopped and I was looking down at her with her head held firmly in my hands.

"I want him gone for good. I want the boys to belong to me completely. You already do, so I'm not adding you into that equation. But I don't like the idea of someone out there who can have any kind of influence in our lives.

Along with that is the burning need inside me to tie you to me in every way possible. I don't fully understand that either, I just know that you gave another man two kids, now you have to give me at least double that."

I think I shocked her into silence because she didn't say anything for a long time. All she did was stare up at me as if she were trying to see into me.

"What if that's not what I want?" Oh boy, here we go. That question sounded like a challenge to me. Something else the little lady under me would have to understand and quickly, is that I won't accept challenges from my woman.

"That's not my fucking problem, every time Laurie, every time I think of him touching you having you, getting you with child it fucking guts me."

This shit even sounded crazy coming out of my mouth, but I'd be fucked if I knew what the hell was going on with me.

"For crying out loud we were kids, it's not like we've been together or anything, he was gone long before the twins were born." She tried getting out from under me but I kept her pinned to the bed with my dick heavy inside her.

"None of that matters don't you understand? I have to wipe him out of your head, I won't be happy until that happens."

I think I tried to do that shit with my dick then, pounding it into her until she sunk her teeth into my chest to bring me back down.

"So what, you want me to get rid of my boys, give them up?" There was all that fire I'd seen that first day. She was pissed and maybe with good reason.

We grappled with each other until I wrestled her onto her stomach, lifted her to where I wanted her, and slammed into her hard from behind.

She bucked and dragged her nails down the mattress as I fucked into her hard while digging the nails of one hand in her hip, and pulling her head back roughly with the other.

"Don't be stupid, the boys are a part of you, he had no hand in raising them. I'm the only father they'll ever know, but you will give me two more just like them, then we'll start on the girls."

"You're insane."
She might be fucking right at that.

Chapter TWELVE

LAURIE

Holy crap he's a barbarian, and not just because of the amount of bruises he left all over me, from his fingers digging into my hips, to the little marks he left all over my neck and breasts. But it was also the way he thinks.

And the things that comes out of his mouth. He'd bought a multi million dollar house one day after meeting us. Maybe that's how things were done in his world, but they certainly weren't the same in mine.

I know he loves the boys, I can see it in his every interaction with them. And they loved him too. There was no shy, hiding behind me, no shunning him the way they did everyone else until they got to know them.

With him it was no holds barred, all out belly laughs, and 'Brett do this and Brett do that.'

Now he's on this thing about Jonathan, a boy I hadn't even given a second thought to since two a.m. feedings eons ago.

He was still pinning me to the bed from our last round of marathon sex. His face was buried in my neck but thankfully he was too tired to maul me again. I don't even want to know what I looked like with all his little love nibbles.

"Am I squashing you love?" He was, but I liked the way it felt, like he was standing between me, and the rest of the world.

"No I'm good."
"Then why do you sound like a strangled hen?" He started to move but I wrapped my legs around him, holding him inside.

"Feeling greedy are you?" He started moving inside me again; he's like a machine.

I like the way he looks into my eyes as he moves, the way he holds my head still while he tells me that he loves me, and most of all I love the way those words make me feel.

If only he could get past this obsession he has with Jonathan, then I think we could maybe possibly have something.

That, and the fact that he seems to have one speed, warp.

***

BRETT

I spent the rest of the day buried inside her until I was raw and she was sore. After licking the soreness away with my tongue, or giving it my best shot, I gave her a bath and then it was time to go get our boys.

"Brett look at me, I can't go outside like this." She was trying to cover up my marks of ownership that were on a couple spots on her neck and her cleavage.

"You stay here and I'll go get them then." I pulled on my jeans and zipped up. I could go for a nap, she'd drained the shit out of me.

"What about tomorrow and the next day? How long do these things last anyway?" she kept rubbing at them like they would go away.

"It doesn't matter sweetheart, because as soon as those fade I'm giving you more."

"You can't be serious."
"It's either that or an engagement ring, and since I know you'd have a fucking fit if I put one of those on you now, it's these for now." I ran my finger over the two in her neck.

I'd be fucked if I'm gonna let her run around without some sign of ownership. It was just my luck that every swinging dick within a five-mile radius would start sniffing around her ass now that I'd found her.

"Are you coming or not?"

"Of course I'm coming you crazy person." At least she was dropping the shy girl act and my little hellion from the park was making a comeback.

"Your ass looks amazing in that thing, go take it off."

"What, what's wrong with it?" She looked over her shoulder at her ass. She was wearing some kind of hot pink, terrycloth number that stopped at her knees, but it hugged her ass like a second skin.

"Put on a skirt, preferably one that reaches the floor."

"Don't be an ass, these pants are perfectly decent."

"Baby." I leaned over so that our eyes would meet. "Go change." Lesson number three; I never fucking argue. It's the worse fucking exercise in futility.

"Brett, this isn't going to work..."

"You've lost your fucking mind." I wasn't even going to give her the chance to finish that asinine fucking statement.

"I told you in the park, if you don't want men looking at your ass don't advertise. Your ass is what caught me by the dick and reeled in the rest of me.

You strike me as smart, so think. Do you really see me being okay with other men enjoying the view? Are you getting where I'm going with this?

And in the future, don't bring up that shit about us not working, because that's not gonna fly, not now, not fifty years from now.

I'm in there and that's just where the fuck I'm staying. Now we're losing time, you need to go change so we can get our boys before they tear those people's fucking place apart."

She hemmed and hawed but since I ignored her ass she had no choice but to do as she was told. I don't think she would've appreciated me getting her dressed myself.

In the end she went with a dress. This long flowing number that wasn't much better. It didn't show her ass off, but it hugged her curves perfectly.

"I'm thinking some of those coverall things farmers wear." She just rolled her eyes and headed out.

I found that I had to keep my hands on her in some way at all times. If I wasn't grabbing onto her nape as we walked, I had my arm around her, resting on her ass as we stood.

The boys were excited to see us and let it be known as they ran to us and started babbling away at us, telling us all about their day.

She kept drawing closer and closer until she was almost under my arm, and when I started to ask her what the hell she was up to, I noticed her giving the women at the center not very nice looks when they got too close.

I pretended not to see shit, but I had a big stupid grin on my face as we left.

Back at the condo she kicked me out of the kitchen to go play with the boys while she cooked. I took them into the study with me and turned on the TV while I looked up some stuff for work.

It was another evening of laughter and little feet running around making my dog crazy, and then it was lights out; my new reality, and so far, so good.

I fucked her, or she fucked me, for half the night, and in the morning, real life intruded and I had to go in to the office.

I tried talking her into staying home again and I had the perfect argument. “Babe, we need to get started on decorating the house, you said you wanted to do it yourself and that’s a big job.

I think you need to devote all your time to it, make sure we get it just the way you want it.”

“Nice try but I’m not about to give up my one source of income and independence.”

“I hate to tell you this babe, but your independence went south five seconds after I fucked you for the first time. Boys quiet down in there.”

She proved to be very stubborn, but since I was ahead by about twelve days, I decided not to push it for now.

I dropped them all off on my way to the office, another part of my new morning routine. "Babe do you drive?"

"I have my license if that's what you mean, but I don't have a car yet."
"We'll get you one, in the meantime you can take the hummer."

"That thing's too big for me to handle."

"Yeah, well the one we're gonna get you isn't gonna be much better, you'll get use to it. It's one of the safest rides on the market."

"I shudder to think what it could possibly be? Does it come with a gun mounted on the top?"

"Thanks for reminding me, I was thinking only of bullet proof glass and shit like that, but a gun mount might be good too."

"It was a joke Cantone, take it easy."

"Uh-huh, we're here." I looked around at the place where she spent eight hours a day five days a week. I knew nothing about it and made a note to myself to find out.

She might not understand her change in life, but I was sure that others, once they find out, will be very aware, and so it was up to me to protect her.

There's no way I can let her stay here. Tonight I'll broach the subject again and try to do it in a way that doesn't raise her hackles.

We shared a hot tongue twister that gave me ideas about turning back for home, and bed, but she pulled away just when my dick was about to get unruly.

"See you later Brett and thanks."

"For what baby?" I caressed her cheek, that needing contact thing again.

"I don't know, for being you I guess."

"You're welcome baby, I love you; see you later." One more smoldering kiss and I went around to help her out of the car.

I watched her ass sway as she walked across the lot and looked around to see who else was looking, and told myself that I really needed to get a grip.

I called her just to mess with her as I pulled out of the parking lot. "I miss you already baby, you sure you don't want to play hooky again?"

"Go to work Cantone, I'll see you later okay. Hey, I think I'm starting to understand those feelings you keep talking about." She hung up before I could say anything.

I started to grin until I heard her voice. At first I thought she was talking to me, but there was something off about the quality in her tone.

'I told you not to do that.'
'Is this why you called out sick yesterday, huh? You little slut, I see you're still up to your sluttish ways. Two kids with no husband aren't enough I see.'
What the fuck?

'Take your hands off me Norm. Do you know how much trouble you can get into if I tell the owner, or worst yet, the labor board?'

'Shit, who's gonna believe you? You're an underage mother, which usually spells slut, while I on the other hand am an upstanding member of the community.'

I could actually see the smirk on the fucker's face as I made a U-turn and headed back to her.

I was lucky enough not to run anyone over, since I wasn't really paying attention to where the fuck I was going.

I slammed on the brakes with my front end nowhere near the curb, and jumped out with my phone still in my hand as I hit the door.

My eyes scanned the area as I heard her in my ear begging this asshole to leave her alone. For the next few seconds my heart was in my throat, especially when I heard what sounded like a slap and a man's voice uttering the words 'you little bitch'.

The place was already packed, but there was no sign of her. I moved towards the back and was in time to see her coming out of a swinging door, holding an apron around her waist while clutching the neck of her torn shirt closed.

Right behind her was a big guy with a greying beard and a beer gut. His tag said manager; that was all I needed.

“Brett?” I ignored her as I reached around her for his fucking neck, pushing him back through the doors into the kitchen.

Everyone seemed to freeze in their tracks as I slammed my fist into his face, knocking him back into the wall.

“Brett, stop it.”

"Get the fuck away from here Laurie." I didn't stop hitting him until my arms were tired and my knuckles hurt like hell. He tried to defend himself but he was no match for my anger.

It was very telling that no one came to his rescue while I beat the shit out of him. And by the time the blood had cleared from my eyes, he was almost comatose.

"You ever come near her again I'll fucking kill you." I dropped him and turned to her. "Get your things you're not staying here."

"Brett."

"Go, now." The asshole on the floor started making blustering noises. "You shut the fuck up unless you want me to finish what the fuck I started."

No one back here had moved as yet, but I could hear raised voices coming from the other side of the door.

"Come here." I pulled her into my chest when she came back with her purse. "You okay?" She nodded her head yes; I pushed her away so I could see her face.

"Don't you dare." She grabbed my suit jacket and refused to let go. "I'm going to kill the son of a bitch." I could see where he had torn her shirt and scratched her in the process.

"Please Brett, for me, leave it alone." If she wasn't here, I would probably end the fuck, but she's a woman with feelings. Begging me for the life of the piece a shit that accosted her.

"Give me your phone, you didn't turn it all the way off by the way, that's how I knew this asshole was hassling you."

I searched through her phone for her dad's number and hit dial. "Chief, no this isn't Laurie, it's Brett Cantone."

"Laurie, the boys..."
"No nothing like that. I need someone down here at the restaurant where she works, her boss just tried to molest her, we're pressing charges."

She looked like she wanted to argue but I quieted her with a look and a kiss to her brow. I'm not the type to let shit like this slide. "It's jail or a wheelchair, choose your pick, but we're not sweeping this shit under the rug."

I'd just dealt with some bullshit of my own, where a female employee, out to make a quick buck, tried to get me for sexual harassment.

When she couldn't get me to fall for that one, she upped the stakes and tried to set me up for date rape. All unbeknownst to me, who just thought I had an overzealous intern on my hands.

Thank fuck I didn't have any interest in her and was never really alone with her, or who knows what might've happened.

That's how I knew that this thing with Laurie was real.

When I met her, I was not in a place where love and relationships were high on my list of priorities. In fact, I was pretty much over the female of the species if I remember correctly.

"Someone will be here soon." We ended up spending all day with that shit because the asshole wanted to press charges for getting the fuck knocked out of his ass.

I didn't give a shit, but my future father in law had a little talk with him that seemed to change his mind.

"We barely have enough time to pick up the boys, we'll order in tonight, you've had a long day."

My adrenaline was still pumping and I knew we still had another round to go, might as well get it over and done with. After today I wasn't leaving anything up to chance.

"You know what this means don't you? You're not going back there."

"Brett don't start that again, he's only one of the managers, the others are nothing like him."

I checked my watch real quick before pulling over to the side. I had six minutes to kill.

"I listened to that fucker manhandling you, it took me more than five minutes to fucking get to you, you really think I'm gonna let you go back there?

"It's my job Brett."
"Fuck this bullshit Laurie; I can buy that place a hundred times over, you don't need to work much less in a place where you were fucking molested.

You know I can take care of you and the boys, you also know that I'm in love with you, if you'd stop being scared long enough to accept it. Think about this shit from my side. Do you really expect me to let you do this shit?"

She didn't say anything, just played with her nails and stared out the window. I wasn't sure if she was thinking over my words or not, but it didn't matter, she had lost all argument when that fucker put hands on her. She'd be lucky if I let her out the fucking house again.

"Time's up, we gotta go get the boys." Was it fair that I was using this fucked up situation to my advantage? Probably not, but hey, she wants to play tough, I'll use whatever the fuck I got.

I didn't let her sulk like she wanted to when we were at home. Instead I dragged her into every conversation I had with the boys.

After dinner I gave them their baths and left her to get them dressed for bed, because I had one more thing I needed to take care of before the day was done.

"Chief, it's me again. Do you know where I can find this Jonathan kid?"

"Why would you be wanting to do that son?"

"I want the boys, I need to meet with him and see how I can make that happen."

"Well now, his name isn't on their birth certificates."

"It isn't?"

"Nope, she was steamed at him for running off, so she didn't acknowledge him."

"Hmm, that's good, but he still knows that they're his and I'd just as soon take care of this now."

"Sure I know where he is, but I still don't see the rush, didn't you and my daughter just meet?"

"Listen, I know you ran me, so you know that in the not too distant future I'm going to put a ring on your daughter's hand whether she wants me to or not."

"Uh, how does that work son?"
"Let's just say we're working on two different timetables, mine's a little faster but not to worry, I have no doubt she'd catch up."

"I have no doubt that you'd see to it that she does."

"This is true, but my point is, when that happens, those two little boys are going to become heirs to one of the biggest fortunes in the land, you get my drift? Not to mention I just don't like the idea of him."

“Oh you’re one of those, good luck son, you’re gonna need it. If you try to corral that little girl, she’ll tear a strip off your hide, I know, I’ve lost a few to that mouth of hers.”

“I don’t think so chief. So you gonna tell me where he is or not?”

He gave me the name of a town that wasn’t that far from here.

“I thought he ran, why so close?”

“He was gone for a while, only came back in the area a couple months ago.”

“And he hasn’t tried to get in touch with her?”

“Nope, he’s not a bad kid, just makes the wrong decisions I think. You’d better let her know what you’re up to because if she finds out later there’ll be hell to pay.”

"I planned to, thanks chief." I hung up and thought about my next move, I needed more information on the kid, first things first; then I'd know what moves to make.

As for telling her, we'll see how it goes. I don't want him anywhere near her so I don't know how I'm gonna pull it off.

Chapter THIRTEEN

Norm the fuck is going to be going away for a good little while, because yes, I'm going to use my money and influence to fry his ass. It's early days yet, but I have it on the best authority that he's fucked.

I'm not sharing any of this with little miss worrywart, but I have to tell her about the errand I'm about to embark on, because after giving it some thought, it's one of those things that I shouldn't keep hidden. I'm not happy about it, but there you have it.

For the past three weeks we've been in the middle of a Mexican standoff. She's pissed because she wants to go back to work, and since she wouldn't take no for an answer, I took the liberty of hiding her shit.

Her dad, after secretly calling me to hear my side, after she'd called him to complain, agrees with me; and so now he's in the doghouse as well. Unlike him, I pay her no damn attention and choose to pretend that all is well.

At night when I pull her under me, she tries giving me the cold shoulder, which lasts for all of two seconds, which is about as long as it takes for me to get her warmed up.

Today I'm taking her to the new house with a fuck load of magazines and paint swatches and some other crap she'd asked me to pick up, but first I have to tell her what I'm up to.

"Babe come here and sit for a minute."

"You'll be late for work." She came and sat with me on the couch in our sitting room while the boys were in our bed watching some sing along crap on the TV.

Since she's staying home she's been keeping the boys with her, and I know she loves it no matter how much she complains.

"What I'm about to say will probably piss you off, before it does just know that nothing I do is ever with the intent to hurt you.

Everything I do now is for all of us, you, me and the boys."

"Oh hell what did you do?" She has the worst opinion of me. I don't know where she gets it.

"Nothing that I know if, but I'm about to do something that I believe is the best course of action for our family."

"I don't like the sounds of this. In the last few weeks you've turned my life upside down. Do you know how incongruous it is for me to move into your house after only knowing you for a few days, or to just leave my job on a whim? Not to mention dragging my boys along with me?"

"Babe, I have an appointment, can you have this meltdown when I get back?" I love those looks she gives me, like she's giving serious thought to hurting me. Too bad she's too short and about half my size.

"Do you know how infuriating it is to never win an argument?"

"I've never argued with you babe so I wouldn't know. Now back to what I was saying. I'm going to meet Jonathan." I braced myself for the argument, but she seemed to be lost for words.

“You called him?” Her voice was deceptively calm, but the pulse beating wildly in her temple gave her away.

“Yes; I knew you would be mad, and judging from what I’ve learned about you in the last three weeks, I knew it would be a waste of time discussing it with you.”

“You had no right.”
“That’s where you’re wrong, I have every fucking right. I claimed you remember, and in so doing I also claimed your sons. This man has a claim to those kids whether you accept it, or I hate it.

Those boys are mine, as you are mine. I’m just going to ensure that there are no surprises in the future. Note I haven’t asked you to take part in this endeavor, that’s because I don’t want you to have anything to do with him.

You haven't seen him in what, four years? I'm thinking there's no need for you to ever see him again."

"If that's the case then why are you even going to see him? Shouldn't I be the one to talk to him? I'm the one he had a relationship with after all."

"You're so cute when you're being funny. By the way, try not to mention you having relationships with other guys, it makes me just a tad fucking nuts."

"For the one hundredth time Brett get a grip. I only slept with the boy once, it was in the back of his car at a drive-in, nothing romantic..."

"You really think it's wise to paint a picture of you in the backseat of some car with this kid minutes before I go to see him? Trust me, I would like nothing better than to off the little bastard..."

"What's he ever done to you?"
"He had you." Fuck I didn't mean to shout that shit.
"Brett seriously, have all your women been virgins?" She was going into one of her snits, tough.

"No, but none of them meant what you do. You think I don't know that I'm acting like a crazy person where that shit is concerned? You think I like being jealous of some fucking kid that I've never even met?

Try seeing this shit from my end would you?"
"Brett, how many times do I have to tell you, there's nothing for you to worry about?"

"In my head I know that babe, but something in me won't let the shit go. I guess I hate the fact that you gave your heart to someone else once before. When I look at you, think of you, I want to own every inch of you. Don't ask me what the fuck that's about because I've never felt anything like it before.

All I know is that I don't want you to ever think of anyone but me ever."

"I don't, I promise. Until we met I never even gave anything like this a thought. I was resigned to keeping my head down and living for my boys until they were old enough and then maybe I would go on with the rest of my life."

"What a fucking waste that would've been baby. I'm glad we found each other, and who knows, maybe after I meet him I'll get over some of this. Anything you want me to say to him?" Not that I was fucking likely to pass it on.

“What could I have to say to him? Now can we get going? You’ve made such a case about me getting started on the house that now I can’t wait to get to it.”

Well now, that answer helped just a little bit to soothe the rough edges around my heart.

“Okay, get the boys ready and we’ll go.” I wasn’t sure about leaving them there alone, but she had decided that today was the day, after three weeks of me badgering her.

We had come a long way in the last three weeks. Solely because I stayed on her ass all day everyday until I got my way. Only because she’s hard headed as fuck and always wants to have her way.

She didn't realize it yet, but she was all mine now, all that was left was getting my ring on her finger as soon as possible. For that I had enlisted the aid of my mother, who was almost as anxious to see us married as I was.

The two of them have met once when I took my new family to meet the rest of the clan. Mom was a bit much, so I figured it was best to expose my girl to her in small doses until I had sealed the deal completely.

For now, they talk on the phone every blessed minute of the day and it's a mixed blessing. I never know what the hell my mother would come up with next and this one is feisty enough as it is without the old woman putting shit in her head, like how to run circles around my ass.

We pulled up to the house and I let them and the dog out, before checking the place over to make sure that everything was safe for them.

"I'll be back to get you for lunch, I'll set the alarm before I go. Don't go wandering around on your own, save that for when I'm here with you."

"Brett, I'm a grown woman, I gave birth to two human beings, would you stop treating me like a baby."

"You're my baby, I don't care what the fuck you've done. Now would you please stay in the damn house until I get back? Come here boys." I knelt so that I could hug them both to me

"Behave for your mom while I'm gone you hear me?" They nodded and babbled at me but I knew they were full of shit.

"Come here you." I pulled her into my arms and sucked her tongue into my mouth. "Love you, now you be good too, and pray that I don't kill this fuck as soon as I see him.

Roll your eyes at me all you want, but you know that shit can happen. See you later."

I'd called this kid a few days ago and asked him to meet me. I hadn't given him much information only that I needed to talk to him about her.

I needed to get this shit over and done once and for all so that I could give her the damn ring I've been schlepping around for the last couple of weeks.

I wanted all three of them to be mine completely and after today, I will make that shit happen. I was prepared to do whatever the fuck it takes to do that shit, well, short of a couple things that I find repulsive.

It was kind of anticlimactic meeting him. It turns out he was just a regular looking kid, who if I didn't know who he was, I wouldn't have noticed.

He was quiet for one, nothing at all like what I envisioned my fiery girl going for.

"Mr. Cantone?"
"Jonathan?" He reached his hand out to shake and I took it. It was funny, but seeing him put me at ease. All the angst and worry I'd been carrying around with me for the last couple of weeks, just seemed stupid as fuck now.

He fixed the glasses on his face and I felt like a heel. Not that he was bad looking, he wasn't, but he just looked so, young. She would've eaten him alive.

I was suddenly feeling very fucking good indeed, and was in a hurry to be done with it and get back to my girl and our boys.

I took a seat across from him at the little table in the food court where he'd asked to meet.

"Like I told you on the phone, this is about Laurie Payne." The poor kid swallowed and looked around like he thought the Feds were going to come get him.

"Relax kid, no one's here to get you. I just want to know what your intentions are where Laurie and the kids are concerned."

Again he swallowed and looked nervous as hell. “What does she want me to do sir?”

“Have you spoken to her since the boys were born, have you seen them?”

“No sir, but I didn’t know what, that is...I didn’t think that she would want me to see them after the way I ran.

I didn’t mean to leave her holding the bag like that I hope she knows that. But my friends said I could go to jail for a long time. My mom even said back then that maybe Laurie would give the baby up for adoption.

I thought that might be best because I didn’t have any way of taking care of them.”

“So you’ve never seen them, never had any interest in seeing them?”

"My friends sometimes see them and tell me how big they're getting and stuff, but Mr. Cantone, sir, I don't think I ever wanted to be a dad. My own dad wasn't very nice if you know what I mean, and I never wanted to be like him ya know, so..."

"So if she got married and her husband wanted to adopt the boys you'd be okay with that?"

"Well, do you know the guy, you said you work for him right? If he's nice I guess I wouldn't mind. If he's going to be good to her and the boys, give them a better life, I guess. I can't do anything for them and that's for sure; and Laurie's a nice girl. I'm sorry I messed up her life."

Damn, I was actually starting to feel sorry for this kid. "I don't think she sees it that way, she loves those boys."

"You still didn't answer me, is he nice?"

"And if he isn't? If I tell you that he's a mean old bastard that will treat them very poorly, but he's loaded, what then?" He actually puffed up his chest and folded his fist.

"Then I'd have to do something. Maybe her dad would help her, he's a cop." I think he was ready to get out the chair and go to battle.

"Are you in love with her?" Can you imagine the fuckery that was going on inside me while I waited for his answer? I'm so fucked in the head I was jealous of whether or not he was in love with my woman.

"No sir, we were just kids playing around. We were friends more than anything else." As usual I made a judgment based on what was in front of my eyes, and my gut.

"What is it that you want to do with your life Jonathan?" I unbuttoned my suit jacket and relaxed back in my seat.

And that's how I ended up spending the next two hours hearing this kid's life story, getting him to sign his kids over to me and cutting him a check for a quarter of a million dollars to start the bike shop he'd always dreamt of owning.

The check wasn't payment, I would never have done such a thing, and surprisingly the kid that had ran out on his pregnant...pal, was not looking to get paid.

No, the money was because he had a need, and because what I was getting in return was worth more than any sum I could've given him.

I walked away knowing that he didn't bear her any great love, that he'd run because of a mixture of bad information and fear, and that at the end of the day, he was an okay guy.

I was glad as fuck that he was headed to the other side of the country though, and that I wasn't going to be seeing him ever again in this lifetime.

I was finally able to breathe easy for the first time in a long while as I climbed into my ride and headed for home.

***

"Well, how did it go?" We were finally in bed back at the condo later that night. The boys had run themselves ragged and were out for the night. Now, it was just she and I.

"You wanna talk about this shit now?" I was busy getting her out of her clothes. I'm surprised she held off this long, but her timing sucked.

"He signed the papers so that I can have the boys. Note I said I, which means you're stuck with me, because they're mine now."

I licked my way down her body until I reached her pussy, which was already starting to get wet. I lifted her to my mouth and licked her clit until it came out of its hood, then teased it gently with the tip of my tongue.

She has lost all inhibitions in bed lately and I have the marks to prove it. She got it into her head that since I mark her she should mark me, and now my back is full of the scrapes from her nails.

"Open for me baby." She spread her legs wider so that my shoulders could fit and I feasted on her.

"Ohhh, Brett..." her voice broke and trailed off just the way I like as she came in my mouth. "Come." I knelt over her and led my cock to her waiting mouth.

The sight of her tits made my cock stand up even harder. "Fuck babe, I want to cum on your tits." But I won't tonight though, oh no, I had more important things to do with my seed.

She licked the head of my cock as she looked up into my eyes. She knows just how to get me going, and when her little hand came up and cupped my balls as she took me all the way back to her throat, I almost lost it.

Fisting her hair, I fucked into her mouth until she choked, then I pulled out of her mouth and mounted her.

"This is the last time we'll discuss him ever again, here or anywhere else."

"Fine, just tell me, are you over whatever the hell that was you had going on?" I fingered her pussy once, twice, to get her juices flowing again, before pulling them out and slamming my dick into her.

"Ahhh." That got her attention. "Yes I am smartass but still the fact remains, you gave him two sons, you'll give me four."

That was the end of the conversation for a while; we both became too caught up in each other.

I pulled her legs higher around my back, bending her in half as I fucked into her hard and deep, trying my best to fuck her into the mattress.

"Give me your mouth."

She was breathing erratically as she turned her lips up to mine. Her body glistened with sweat as she moved beneath me wildly.

"I you love you Brett."
"I know sweet girl I know." I reached over, sending my cock deeper into her belly as I opened the nightstand drawer and removed the little velvet and leather box that I kept there.

I never stopped moving inside her as I retrieved the ring with my teeth and dropped it on her chest.

Leaning on one arm I took it in the other. "Give me your hand." She didn't hesitate, but lifted her hand for me to slip the ring on her finger.

I pounded harder and harder into her as she clenched around me, while I bit down on the ring I'd just bonded her with. "By the way, I changed your pills weeks ago." And with that I pushed through her cervix and released my seed.

Chapter FOURTEEN

LAURIE

"Brett, are you trying to impregnate me, or kill me?" I could barely get the words out because I was still breathing like a runaway train.

"What, why, am I too heavy?"
"No." I squeezed my thighs around his hips so he'd know that that wasn't it. I love feeling his weight on me, pressing me down, after we've made love. It adds an extra special something.

When he could move he lifted his head from its favorite spot in my neck, to look down at me.

"Then what is it?" He started moving inside me again.

"That." I pinched his ass, because seriously, he was too much. I don't know where he got it into his head that we have to have sex every hour on the hour for me to get pregnant, but the last time I reminded him that I got that way the first time after only one try, the house was like a deep freeze for days. He's so touchy about certain things.

"We've been in this bed for four days, we've only left long enough to eat."

"And?" At least we were having fun while we were at it, because I seriously believe that it was his intentions to keep me here until the job was done.

It's been a month since he sprang his little surprise about the pills on me. At first I thought he was joking, I mean I would've noticed if my pills had been switched out wouldn't I?

But in the morning when I checked, which was the first time he let me out of bed by the way, he sure had changed them. I'd been popping vitamins since we moved in.

I tried getting him to see just how wrong he was for that, but have you ever tried arguing with a tree stump? Yeah, it's about the same. Only I think the stump might give you something, not Brett.

It was only after his mom and I grew closer, and I had an ally that I came to understand him.

Brett, to put it mildly, is spoilt. And now he's leading my boys down the same path. As a single teenage mom, I know tough, or at least I thought I did. I hadn't run into anything like him before though.

He takes charge of everything without asking, and how he knows what I need is sometimes a mystery, because I try not to ask him for anything.

With Brett more is always better. Which is why I'm surprised that he lct me have my garden wedding two weeks ago at our new home, instead of the massive do his mother wanted to plan.

I finally figured it out. He was trying to make up for all he thinks I've missed out on, which is sweet, but unnecessary.

I also figured out how to deal with his brand of nutty. If he thinks something is harmful or can be potentially harmful, there's no moving him. But if it's just something I want or need, he'd move heaven and earth to get it for me.

Let's not get started on the boys. I think we now own the equivalent of two toy stores.

After that day when he came back with the papers, nothing would do but that he adopt the boys right away.

To do that he said, we first had to get married. I begged him to get a pre-nuptial agreement, I knew what most people were going to think after all; but his words were and I quote, 'where the fuck you gonna go?'

Now he's had me in this bed for days it feels like. From the minute dad took the boys on a camping trip with their new uncles and grandfather, which is what Brett's dad said they should call him.

I should probably tell him that he'd already done the deal, long before I even knew that he'd changed my pills, but I needed just a few more days of peace and quiet. I knew that as soon as I say those words my life, as I know it, is over.

"It's not my fault that your pussy feels this good. It's like you did something to it, it's hotter inside and the walls feel different."

It can't be, "really?" I moved with him now because I couldn't help myself. He has this way of making me just as hungry for him as he is for me, no matter how worn out I might be.

"Yes really, I stay hard inside you haven't you noticed? So in essence it's you who've been keeping me in bed all this time. When I'm not in you I'm thinking of being in you. And when I do get inside you, I can't leave. I think you bewitched me."

Yeah that's it alright. I think for the sake of my sanity and my sore girly bits I'd better tell him; heaven help us.

"Brett?" I ran my hands soothingly down his back.
"Yeah?" I almost couldn't get my thoughts together because he was still moving inside me. Only this time it was slow and easy, instead of the pounding lust that we'd shared just a short while ago.

"I have something to tell you."
"What is it?" He pulled his head back again. How can he look so relaxed when he was making me crazy?

Here goes, "I'm pregnant." He stopped all movement and just stared down at me for a full minute.

"You sure?" His voice was as soft as I'd ever heard it; there was such reverence in it.

"What're you doing?" he pulled out of my body and laid between my thighs.
"I want to see." What could I do but roll my eyes at that? There was nothing to see, not yet anyway.

But I endured his thorough inspection until he'd satisfied himself that there was nothing to see as yet, then he slid back into me and we made love for the rest of the afternoon. I guess it wasn't just about breeding me after all.

BRETT

"Mom, I know what you're going to say, but here's the deal. My wife is not going anywhere for the weekend without me. I don't know whatever gave you the idea that I would go for this."

“Brett, it’s not the weekend it’s just one night. We’ll go to the show and dinner and be back first thing in the morning.”

“Take your husband with you, he likes that opera crap.”

“But it’s girls night.”

“Her girls night is going to be right here in this house. If she wants to see the Pirates of Penzance I can rent the movie.”

“It’s not the same thing and you know it.”

“Oh well. Did she put you up to this? Tell me she didn’t.”

“No, she said you’d never go for it so don’t even try, but I thought for sure that if you knew she wanted to see it that you’d let her have her way.”

"And she can see it, I'll even sit through the crap when it comes here."
"But that won't be for months."

"So? Mom get a grip, you know just as well as I do that there's no way I'm letting my pregnant wife go off anywhere where I can't keep an eye on her." They didn't need to know that I had more tags on my family than the pentagon had on the president; that would only defeat the purpose after all.

The women in this family are about as sneaky as they come. Too bad I'm always one step ahead of them. In the two months since she told me she was carrying my child, she's been trying to make me crazy.

In all fairness it wasn't anything she was doing, it's just that I find it hard to go on with my day when all I do is worry about something going wrong.

My father in law and even my own dad seems to think that I'm a lost cause. According to their archaic memories, neither of them had the same issues I now suffer from.

Like jumping up in the middle of the night in a cold sweat because you just knew you were going to get it wrong.

Second-guessing everything. Staying up for hours trying to plan for what comes next.

Right now I'm trying to spend as much time with the boys as possible so that when the baby comes there's no conflict.

I've been reading up on that shit a lot, because although this child was the first of my loins, those two will always be my firstborns.

I know that Laurie needs that security for them, that a big part of her problem in the beginning was accepting that a man could want to claim her boys as their own.

Since the adoption, I've done everything in my power to reassure her and I know it's gone a long way to making her happy.

Now all I need is to get through this pregnancy with my sanity intact and we're good to go. I had no idea this shit was going to turn my life upside down the way it has.

"I can't talk to you." She flounced up out of the chair and headed for the door.

"Fine, who's next in the lineup?" She didn't bother to answer, which means she's pissed. I don't see why, I'm pretty sure she knew before she came into my study what the answer was going to be. Just as she'd known each time she'd asked me about one of their hair-brained schemes in the past.

"Boy, what did you do to your mom, she's steamed?"

"I don't see why; you two got anything else on the agenda for today? Because I really need to get some work done. The boys were in here two minutes before she was, telling me all about some new toy dad brought them.

The object of me working from home was that I'd actually get some work done instead of worrying about you all the time."

"Cantone, look at me."

I looked up at her and felt my heart melt the way it always does. "I'm looking."

"I don't even have a tummy yet, but you're already making everyone crazy." I looked out the windows like I was searching for something.

"What're you doing?"
"I'm trying to see whose house we're at."
"And what's that supposed to mean?"

"It means that if anyone doesn't like what I'm doing, they're always free to go, and no before you ask, that does not include you.

Why don't you and that old lady knit a blanket or something, whatever happened with that?"

"We can't knit all day everyday Brett. Sometimes you need to get out the house, get some fresh air, spread your wings."

Again I looked out the window and she sighed.
"What're you doing now?"

"There's about five acres of land out there, all within the safety of the thick ass walls that surround this place. Take Gunther with you if you can't wait 'til I'm done here.

I grinned to myself when she too got up and flounced out of the room. My ass she's going away for the night, I wouldn't sleep a fucking wink. I hardly sleep as it is and she's right next to me. No way.

I don't care what anyone in this family says, it's not abnormal for a man to want to keep on top of his pregnant wife every second of the day.

When I was trying to seed her, I wasn't actually thinking about this part of things. I basically saw my dick going in, doing its thing, and then a little being that looked like the boys coming out.

Women talk a lot of shit about what it feels like to be pregnant. I'll stick my neck out there and say they don't know the half of it.

They're not the ones who have to worry about what's going on inside her body when you're not there to watch over the two of them.

They don't break out in a sweat because your whole life is walking around in a five three package that weighs maybe a hundred pounds.

They don't sit around contemplating the fact that her womb is like the most precious thing in your world for the next however long the kid decides to stay in there.

That instead of one, you now worry for two, every time she's out of your sight. Or how the thought of all the pain you keep hearing is awaiting her makes you wish you'd never touched her, until the next time you bury yourself inside her of course.

How do you let your most prized possession, the thing you hold most dear, out of your fucking sight, without going crazy?

Don't get me started on the dangers that no one tells you about. The shit that has you afraid that she'd stub her fucking toe if you're not there to hold her hand.

I know I've lost my shit I don't need anyone to tell me. I just need them to let me get through the next six months in my own way.

Too bad I know that shit isn't about to happen, just as I know I'm not going to breathe easy again in this lifetime. This love shit is a racket.

EPILOGUE

"Dmitri, Garrett, cut that shit out right now."
"Yes daddy." They chorused together, little hardheaded fucks. I've told them three times already about jumping off the top bunk of their beds.

Why the hell they each needed a bunk bed was beyond me, but their mother said some shit about sleepovers. All they did was use the shits to do stunts; then again that's the way they treat everything.

They've grown like tumbleweeds in the last few months and if you don't keep an eye on them, they can destroy Abbottabad in ten minutes flat.

After peeping around the corner of their room door to assess the damage, I headed to the master suite and the other pain in my ass.

Shit has been shifting around here of late, and I've only just come to realize it. It happened when I woke up one morning and there was a new roundness to her tummy.

Yes, I am still into cataloguing my feelings about shit where she's concerned, and I can still remember my every emotion at the discovery.

Joy, fear, crippling fear, love, reverence and a whole lot of fuck me what am I going to do now?

It's not a good thing when a strong man gets brought to his knees. It's especially fucked when your whole family, including your new father in law the badass cop, watches you like you're out of your fucking mind.

I have a whole new respect for the men I see walking beside their blossoming wives. I know how it feels to be down in the trenches.

In fact I have met quite a few in our Lamaze class and the other five or so classes I made her sign up for, no matter how much she complains that she's already done this blah-blah-blah.

We've formed a kind of support group, because as far as I can see, there're hundreds of those shits for the females and none for men.

Like our contribution ends at fucking ejaculation! I mean to have my place in this pregnancy thing, do my part to make life as easy as possible for her, even though she complains that my hovering is doing the complete opposite.

I've even been training the boys to do their part. Gunther, forget about it. I don't know how the fuck he knows, but he's on her like white on rice whenever I'm not around.

I made it through morning sickness by the skin of my fucking teeth and never wish to go through that shit again.

The only good thing about it is that I was the one who actually felt it, she just skated by with a few little blips; but it was daddy over the fucking john every morning like a sap.

You can imagine the fun the men in my family had with that one. After that fuckery it was her cravings. It was hard to keep up with those shits, because as soon as you thought you had them figured out, she hit you with a new one at two o'clock in the damn morning when everything is closed.

"How you feeling baby? What are you grinning at?" she was relaxing back against a mountain of pillows just the way I like to see her.
"It's so cute the way they call you daddy, without us even prompting them to."

"I'm their father, what the fuck you want them to call me?" I was thrilled as fuck about that turn of events myself. I never really gave much thought to what they were going to call me as long as they were mine I was fine.

But I'll never forget the day little Dmitri called me daddy for the first time. It had been so effortless, and he'd just gone about his business as though he hadn't just rocked my world off its axis. It was just as I would've wanted it to be if I had a choice.

She rolled her eyes at me and rubbed her overly large tummy.

"Hey you in there, don't be like your dad and brothers, please have a little humility."

"Don't be telling my boys that shit." I straddled her and put my mouth to her stomach, speaking to my kids the way I've been doing since her fifth month.

"Hey boys this is daddy, you be good for your momma today, no aerobics against her ribs yeah." I kissed her tummy and eyed her thoughtfully after imparting some more words of wisdom to the young Cantones.

"Don't even think about it, you had some this morning, besides the hooligans are up and about."

"They're busy trying to kill themselves and each other." I eyed her tits as I stroked my hardening cock through my shorts.

“Brett no.” she laughed and tried to roll away from me but she wasn’t quick enough.
"I'll be quick."

"Brett."
"Ssh." I pulled her to the edge of the bed and pushed her dress up under her chin so I could suck on her sensitive nipples while I stroked it.

"Spread babe."
She opened her legs wider and I put two thick, long fingers in her pussy to get her juices flowing.

After a few strokes of my fingers in her heat with her nipple in my mouth, she was primed for it. “Cum on my hand baby.” I hit the clit and she went off.

Licking my fingers clean I lined up my cock and went in, my eyes closing in pleasure. I pulled her legs up high in the air and bent my knees so I could dig deep.

I smiled and looked deeply into her eyes as I slid all the way home, as I ran my hands over my two little ones in her belly.

Turns out multiples run in her family and she was some kind of phenomenon because she was having a second set.

I'd told her they were going to be even more amazed when I fucked another set in her three months after these two were born.

"Fuck, your pussy's so fucking hot; clutch my dick baby, yeah just like that." Shit now I'm in trouble.

I felt my balls draw up as I got ready to shoot too soon, fuck, but lately that's the way it's been, as soon as I got inside her I lost it.

It was the kids in her womb, my kids my seed. That more than anything said I owned her, that this woman was mine, a part of me was growing inside her. The thought makes me lose my shit every time.

Reaching down between us I played with her clit.
"You love my cock don't you little girl?"

I found out quite by accident that dirty talk is one of her trigger; it works to send her over every time.

Leaning in, I bit her ear, before whispering to her as I stroked into her.

"Later, when the boys are asleep, I'm gonna eat your sweet pussy from behind would you like that?"

"Fucccccckkkkk."
Uh huh she went off like a firecracker; at least she didn't scream it this time.

She was out like a light by the time I pulled out of her, which is just perfect. It's the only time I ever get any real peace these days, when she's asleep.

***

Four Months Later

"Brett the kids."
"They're fine, they're watching Barney that'll give me half an hour at least to off load in you."

"But what if one of them come looking for us?"

I was busy herding her into our bedroom while she fretted.

"Then I'll just explain that daddy's giving mommy her medicine." It had been hours since I'd had her and I'm still on my bi-hourly feedings.

I laid her on the bed as gently as I could since she was roughly the size of one of grandpa's prize horses. When she was comfortable on her side I put a pillow under her and climbed up between her legs.

"It's all your fault anyway, you know what the sight of your pregnant ass does to me." It's true, instead of my lust burning out from too much contact it seemed to grow more and more.

I guess I'm lucky that she's right there with me, that she's always as hungry for me as I am for her. And those rare times when she's not, I get almost as much pleasure from playing with her body, discovering all the newness since the last time I'd inspected her.

I teased her first, rubbing my cock over her clit and slit, chewing softly on her nipples, until she was begging to be fucked.

"Please Brett just put it in, stop torturing me." My dick was hard as fuck as I slid it into her at an angle. I stay out of her cervix these days because she's really sensitive, but I get as far as I can inside her without hurting her.

"Damn feel them go." I could feel the babies doing their exercise routine in her womb as I moved in and out of her. The love I felt for her in that moment could not be contained.

"Look at me, I love you sweetheart." She smiled and clenched around me as I fucked her nice and slow. No rough fucking for my girl while she was breeding.

"You stay in here and get some rest I've got the boys." I looked back at her as she tried to catch her breath. Maybe I shouldn't have done that.

She was past the date they'd given her for delivery, since she wasn't supposed to go full term with twins, especially not a second set.

She was close to thirty-four weeks and counting. "I can feel you staring, I'm fine go be with the boys." I couldn't resist going back for one more kiss, before fixing the sheet around her and leaving the room.

I knew it; from the minute I left her I knew, so when Gunther started barking seconds before she screamed I wasn't too surprised.

I had to calm our boys before I could go to her, because that scream had scared even me.

"Okay baby I'm right here." I helped her sit up on the side of the bed before going to the chair where we had her hospital clothes already laid out.

I was coolheaded, gave the boys instructions on how to hit the right button to get grandma and then grandpa.

There had been a lot of debate as to what we should do with the boys when this day came. Thankfully it was only seven in the evening and not the middle of the night like I'd been expecting.

In the end I wanted them there with us, the others were going to meet us there and when they had to come home later then mom would bring them back here.

My movements were methodical since I'd spent many hours going over this shit in my head. "Come baby." Even my voice sounded calm and relaxed, like we were going on one of our many family outings.

I held her hand in mine all the way, while fielding questions from the boys who were very excited to finally meet their new playmates.

I made it through the signing in and the prepping, I was even congratulating myself. I couldn't wait to tell the other dads to be what a cakewalk it all was after all the hype.

But then she was crying and screaming and nothing was being done about that shit. “Give her something you fucks.”

“It’s too late Mr. Cantone your wife chose to forego the Demerol and now she’s in the middle of labor it can’t be administered.”

“What the fuck...”
“Brett.” She squeezed my hand. “It’s okay just stay with me.” I don’t know how it happened, maybe I wished it, whatever the case, the next time that little machine announced a contraction, I ended up on my knees next to her bed with a burning tearing pain in my gut.

It was like the room went still including her and all eyes were on me. “What the fuck was that?”

"You'd better lay down Mr. Cantone." I started to answer the doctor but another one of those things hit me out of nowhere and cut off my air.

She was laughing, unbelievable. "Baby." They tried to get me to lie down but I wasn't leaving her no matter what.

"I knew you would find a way Brett I just couldn't figure out how." I'm glad somebody was enjoying this shit. It felt like I had hot spikes boring holes in my gut.

I was man enough to make it through the birth of my sons, even though I felt like I would keel over any minute, I stood firm, wiped her brow, let her rip my arm out the fucking socket, and kept the nausea that was riding my ass hard, at bay.

Where I finally lost my shit is when the fucking asshole doctor that has been telling me for the last eight months or so that she has everything under control uttered the words 'what do we have here?"

Who the fuck wants to hear that shit at a time like this? I was imagining all kinds of shit as I stood there with a kid in each arm, about to pass them off to their mother who was about to smile, before her face screwed up and she screamed like somebody gut punched her.

"What's wrong with her, what the fuck did you do?"

"Calm down Mr. Cantone everything's still okay here. It just appears that there's another uh..."

"Another what? What's going on?" I didn't know what to do so I ended up placing the kids on the bed next to her so I could take her hand as she started pushing again.

I was trying to remember this part in all the books I'd read but kept coming up empty.

Laurie wasn't talking, she was too busy screaming in between breaths and the fucking personnel were running around the room like we had an emergency.

"Somebody tell me what the fuck is going on." I heard my family beyond the door, probably alerted by my yelling, and then everything happened at once.

Another little cry rent the air and my eyes flew right to ground zero where the all but fucking dead doctor was holding up a third bundle.

I lost all sense of self, time and place. There was a ringing in my ears and I was very close to passing the fuck out. I held firm though, until she said the words ' congratulations, you have a daughter'.

It's a good thing I wasn't holding the boys because no one was in time to break my fall when I landed.

THE END

***

Made in the USA
Las Vegas, NV
20 October 2023